TELL ME HOW IT WAS

AN ANTHOLOGY OF IMAGINED
MICHIGAN HISTORIES

MG Press
http://midwestgothic.com/mgpress

Tell Me How It Was © 2015 by MG Press and 826michigan. All rights reserved MG Press. No portion of this book may be reprinted in any form, print or electronic, without written permission, except in the case of brief quotations embodied in critical articles and reviews.

ISBN: 978-0-9882013-6-1

Cover design © 2015 Lauren Crawford

Cover photo © Silas Grimes

TELL ME HOW IT WAS

AN ANTHOLOGY OF IMAGINED
MICHIGAN HISTORIES

From the eighth-grade writers of
Scarlett Middle School

Foreword i
Introduction iii

1999

January 2, Jalen Walker 1
January 4, Inayah Amir Bey 9
January 4, Olivia Figueroa 13
October 14, Michael A. Zamborowski 17

2001

January 28, Rami Emad Breadiy 20
June 28, Terrence A. Vick II 25
August 24, Kiara Jones 27
September 11, Ricardo Mojica 31
September 11, Michael Pocrnich 33
September 11, Viola Cole 37
September 18, Richarra Roach 45

2005

July 9, Fatima Ali-Khodja 51
July 12, Sofie Gelderloos 59
August 20, Ethan Lichtenberg 62
August 22, Jafiah Edwards 65
August 28, Ari Barajas 69
November 18, Odia Kaba 72

2008

September 3, Anthony Van 74
November 3, James Cardwell. 80
November 11, Derek Berger 84

2012

February 5, Ian Barritt 87
February 10, Serenity Hill 91
October 22, Lochlann Dunlavey 97
October 23, Eric Salazar 100
October 28, Anastasia Roberson 101
December 21, Bryan Carmona 103
December 21, Michael Rosas-Martinez 107
December 22, Adriana Gonzalez-Figueroa 110

Acknowledgments 115
About MG Press 116
About 826michigan 117

FOREWORD
Rebecca Scherm

When we read, we're looking to experience, for a time, life as someone else. We want to zip on someone else's human-suit and have a look around at the world as they see it. If that's why we read, that's also why some of us are drawn to write: there are people we can only imagine, and we are curious to become them, even just for a little while.

To write historical fiction is to inhabit not just another person, but another time—the world as we might never have known it. For the student writers creating historical fiction in this anthology, the worlds they are inhabiting in these stories are often just beyond the reach of their memories. And yet writing from these perspectives helps us all, writers and our readers, to understand how our changing environments shape our perceptions of the world.

In many of these stories, the current events that define the year in our history books are far removed from everyday life, as they are for most of us: one student writer imagines an ordinary day gone terribly awry on the eve of President Obama's election. In other stories, cultural events give the characters' lives a texture that grounds them in time: the release of *Harry Potter and the Goblet of Fire*, the tragic death of Whitney Houston. And yet other writers reach into historical events like we might grope around a dark room, looking for a light switch: one story imagines the awful uncertainty of missing family in the immediate aftermath of Hurricane Katrina; another witnesses the events of September 11, 2001 on television, but as an adult whose flight into New York was delayed that day.

If the goal of reading and writing fiction is to allow us to simultaneously escape—ourselves, our lives, the present day—and to connect with others beyond our reach, these young writers are doing that hard, rewarding, and sometimes sublime work of imagining lives outside their own. Read these stories and time travel with them.

INTRODUCTION

Catherine Calabro, Frances Martin, and Hannah Rose Neuhauser of 826michigan

You may not realize it, but this book is a convergence of midwestern might: a collaboration between MG Press, 826michigan, and Scarlett Middle School that will go down in history.

MG Press came to 826michigan in the fall of 2014 with an intriguing proposal: the press was interested in creating a publication that would celebrate the young generation of writers in the midwest. 826michigan knew just where to turn: students at Scarlett Middle School and their English Language Arts (ELA) teachers, Sal Barrientes and Ellen Daniel.

Sal and Ellen shared plans for their upcoming historical fiction unit and posed a challenge to the group: could we create a writing workshop that allowed students to engage with recent historical events in an imaginative way?

With the support of 826michigan volunteers, Robert James Russell of MG Press led the students through three sessions of historical exploration and fiction writing exercises. The students explored the genre conventions of historical fiction and were encouraged to bend the rules of this genre. The students researched the recent past, learning about unexplainable trends (beanie babies) and obsolete technologies (GameBoy Colors). They learned about major events including Y2K, the advent of Facebook, and President Obama's election, and delved into the details of large-scale tragedies from Hurricane Katrina to 9/11 to imagine stories that would make these important historical events real and new to readers.

Students chose places in Michigan important to them to serve as their settings and created characters to explore the events and spaces of the recent past. The conflicts of the stories revolve in some way around the setting—place and/or time—and illuminate not only a human experience of this period, but also these young writers' understanding of events that happened just before their conscious memory. The results are a captivating anthology of imagined local histories—some pieces have elements of magical realism and others stick to a stricter interpretation of the past. All of the stories illustrate how history can be given new dimension and be reinterpreted through the minds' of these young writers.

The writers of Scarlett Middle School have brought their grit and originality to this work, exploring history in a new and nontraditional way. And thus was born Imagined History: short, place-based, modern historical fiction, a truly uncharted genre and one we are excited to share with you today.

1999

JANUARY 2

Jalen Walker
Age 13

"A-alright, s-see you guys later, love you," Kyoko said, leaving out the door. As she closed the door, a zipper on her backpack got caught and all of her books fell to the snow-covered ground. After she dropped her books, her glasses tumbled from her face as she was looking down at the books. Now, she could barely see anything, so she started patting the ground to find them. When she found them, she looked at her watch and quickly picked up her things and started running to the bus stop. She was late!

When she got to the bus stop, the doors had already closed and it was ready to leave, but she and the bus driver, Patty Civils, were very close, so the doors swung back open and Kyoko, as always, heard Patty's laughing sing-song, "Better luck next time, dolly." Patty was a southern gal, and she understood Kyoko, because she was an orphan, too. The bus finally got to the school, Huron High School.

She walked in the school and started walking toward her first class. As she was hurrying down the corridor, she heard a girl talking about her, saying, "It's so sad to be that ugly. I wish I could give her money to get plastic surgery. And . . ." she stopped as she caught sight of Kyoko but it was too late. Kyoko walked up to her and slapped her across the face and walked away.

She was at her locker and saw her best friend, Andrew.

"That wasn't very nice you know, you could have dealt with it another way," he said

"I know now, but at that minute I was just really mad, and isn't it better to get your anger out, right then and there?" Kyoko said.

"Not like that," he replied, though he was giggling. "I really think you should try to stop being so hot-headed."

"I can try but I don't think I can conceal all of . . . "

Just then, she heard over the speaker *Kyoko Kyles, report to the office now; Kyoko Kyles, to the office*. She looked down the hallway and saw the girl that she had just slapped across the face, smiling an evil and wicked smile. Kyoko's face turned pale and her eyes lit up.

Andrew looked sadly at her: "I told you." He closed his locker and headed to class.

Kyoko got to the office and checked in with the secretary. She didn't even have time to sit down to wait. She saw the principal standing at the door to her office. The principal was very gullible, so she believed the girl. Not to mention, the girl was the principal's daughter.

"Now Kyoko, please do explain why you punched Amanda in the face," the principal said.

"I slapped her, not punched. And I apologize for that."

"Why would Amanda lie to me? What good would that do her? She told me that you punched her in the face after she tried to be nice and say hello."

Kyoko heard something that sounded like a fake sob. She looked over and saw Amanda covering up the half of her face that the principal could see, the other side smiling at Kyoko, all while acting like she was crying.

"I'll be calling your aunt about this later and will tell her that you are suspended for two days. Now this will never happen again, will it?" the principal said.

Kyoko looked at her with astonishment. Since she didn't want to make the case worse for herself, she just simply shook her head.

"You may go," the principal said.

She walked out of the office and saw Andrew waiting for her. He had all of her things for class. "You okay, Ko-Ko?" he asked.

"Well, I got suspended because of that little brat. But it's not like it's the first time," Kyoko said, starting to walk.

"How long this time?" he said. "One, two, three days? Let me guess, um, two days."

"Two is the principal's favorite number!" they said together, while bursting in laughter.

Kyoko saw him later on at the end of the day, talking to their friend Simon. She walked over to them and looked down to see if anything had changed. As always, something had; Simon had a new pair of Converse. "I didn't know there were that many pairs of Converse in the world; you should stop buying so many before your family goes bankrupt," she said, while starting to laugh, but she knew that would never happen since his family was almost rich.

"Haha, very funny, but when you're this cool, you have to show everyone how cool you are," Simon said with a smirk on his face.

"I don't think it's humanly possible for you to be cool. You can dream though," Andrew said.

"Haha, but see you guys later. I have to be home for some family dinner," Simon said.

While Simon was running to his car, Kyoko and Andrew were walking to Andrew's. He drove a Ford truck that was black with red stripes. Andrew gave her a ride home every day. They got in and, as always, his leather seats made the most loud and annoying sound: *Screeeech*. It was a loud kind of screechy sound. They saw snow on the window; it had been a cold winter. A few days back, there was a big snow storm.

Kyoko looked at Andrew with a questioning face. "Can't you get new seats or something? I know you don't like the sound either," Kyoko said waiting for an answer.

Andrew looked back at her, "Never. I refuse to get new seats. These seats are ancient, who would sell something ancient?"

Kyoko's lip dropped in astonishment. Then she started laughing, "You're so mean—even though your parents drove this car that doesn't make it ancient."

"Yes, it does. They're like forty, so yeah, it's ancient," Andrew said surprisingly with a straight face.

"Oh okay, I'll just tell your mom and dad how ancient you think they are," Kyoko said, starting to laugh.

Laughing and shaking his head, Andrew said, "Anyway, do you want to come over today? My family is getting some Chinese food."

"That sounds awesome, but I have to go get killed by my aunt. You know how I got suspended."

"Oh yeah, maybe another time."

He drove off into the street and started on the route to Kyoko's house. When they got there, Kyoko remembered that her little brother Jinhai had a half day today. She jumped out of the car and said, "Bye Drew," closed the door behind her, and ran into the house to see her brother.

When she got in, she saw her aunt at the stove cooking dinner. "Hey, I'm just gonna walk out before you yell at me," she said, starting to walk away slowly while taking off her white winter coat. "Nothing happened; I just want to go see my brother so, um, bye now."

"He went to the park, and what in the world are you talking about?" Her aunt was the sister of her father; the only reason she was taking care of them was because Kyoko's parents died when she was nine. For years, Kyoko thought it was her fault because they got in the car accident on the way to get her a new toy from the store. She cried herself to sleep every night until she was twelve.

Starting to get worried that she was going to get yelled at, she said, "I'm gonna go to the park, bye."

When she got to the park, she saw one of his friends, but not him. She went to the friend and asked, "What are you guys doing, hide and seek?"

"Yeah, but today they're hiding really well!" the little boy said.

Kyoko heard a scream; it sounded like her brother. She ran in the direction of the scream. She saw a man holding her brother, about to throw him into a car. Kyoko felt a fire start up inside her—her little brother Jinhai and her aunt were the only things she couldn't lose.

Kyoko dashed furiously at the man. She kicked him in the jaw and almost broke it. She got Jinhai and asked him if he was okay. Then she took the guy by the shirt and said, "If you EVER touch my little brother again, I will personally throw you off the face of the earth. GOT IT?!"

"A-alright," the man said.

She looked back at the kids; they looked astonished. "Cooooooool!" all of the kids said. She would have laughed, but she was too angry. When she was this angry growing up, the only one who could calm her down was Andrew. Jinhai took Kyoko's phone out of her pocket and dialed him up, and said, "Hey Andrew, this is Jinhai. It's a 904 this time, really bad." 904 meant she was really mad, so you can imagine.

"Oh my, I'm leaving now."

When he got there she was sitting on a swing, swinging back and forth with her long black hair in her face and her fist balled. He walked over, sat on the swing next to her, and asked, "Are you okay ma'am, because in a second, we're going to have ask you to leave the premises."

Kyoko laughed, "Oh, shut up." She looked up at him. "Jinhai called you, didn't he?"

"Yeah, he did."

Looking at her for a while, he noticed something in her backpack. It was a new Game Boy. "Woah! How did you get one of these, and who for? I know you don't like playing video games." Game Boys were really popular in Michigan during this time.

"I've been saving up for my brother. It took a while but I finally had enough."

Right after that it started raining; it was always raining in Michigan. Kyoko smiled—she loved the rain. Andrew smiled looking at Kyoko. He had been in love with her since third grade.

"Why are you looking like that? You're smiling really hard and blushing," she said, tapping his nose and laughing. "Awwww, it's adorable!"

Andrew kissed her. He thought to himself, *I'm tired of waiting*. And in that moment, Kyoko for the first time in a long time, felt at home.

JANUARY 4

Inayah Amir Bey
Age 13

This was the day she was waiting for: Aspynn was going to get her favorite game. Aspynn's mother and father had left to see family in Japan just a couple days earlier (though her father was from Cuba). In Japan, the Pokémon games had already been released, but in America, the game was not yet released. In advance, Aspynn asked—more like begged—her mother to get her favorite game, Pokemon Green, as a present from Japan, even though she had yet to play it. Luckily, her mother taught her and her twin brother Steven Kanji, Hiragana, and Katakana, so she would have no problem reading the Japanese text in her game.

"Aspynn! Mom is on the phone!" her brother Steven called to her as she came downstairs.

"Thanks," she said, grabbing the home phone from her brother. Aspynn and her brother had a very strong relationship. It was the morning of January fourth, and all she had to do was get through school and then she could finally get her game, and she was excited that her mother and father were coming back from Japan. They had left a week earlier and left the twins with their grandmother.

"Hi Mom. How are you?" Aspynn asked her mother through the phone, taking a seat on the living room couch next to her brother.

"Hi Aspynn. I'm fine. How's your brother and grandmother?" she asked in a very strong Japanese accent.

"Just fine. It looks like we have a snow day here in Michigan. Will you be able to catch your flight?"

"Your father and I will have to stay here until the storm passes. I will call later on today. Don't get into any trouble and listen to your grandmother."

"Mom, we know, we know. Love you. Bye," Aspynn said as she hung up the home phone and put it back on the charging dock.

"Great. Just great." Aspynn said, slumping down on the couch. "I've waited forever for Mom and Dad to get back, not only just to see them and hear about our family, but it's gonna be *soooooo* long until we experience the Pokémon life. So what are we going to do if there's no school and almost two feet of snow on the ground outside while our grandma is still snuggled up in bed?" Aspynn asked her brother, staring at the television, watching the school closings and weather.

"You thinking what I'm thinking?" Steven asked turning his head to look at his sister.

"No, not really," she responded, looking right back at him.

Steven sighed, "And to think that we're twins."

"Grandma, Steven and I are going outside, alright?" Aspynn told her grandmother.

"Okay. Be careful, and tell me if you're going on a walk or what not," their grandmother said sweetly.

"Okay, so what do we do now?" Aspynn said cluelessly to her brother who was dressed in heavy, warm layers because of the cold and snowy weather, in the front yard of their house.

"We have fun. You wanna sit inside all day and play, and watch cartoons all day until your brain rots, or have fun with your brother?"

"I guess I will spend my precious time with my brother but what are we gonna do? Two fifteen-year-olds who start a snowball fi—" she stopped mid sentence as a snowball collided with her face.

"Yep. Right on. You gonna play or wha—" then a snowball collided with his face.

"You're on." Aspynn said, slowly backing away.

* * *

"I definitely won," Aspynn said, sitting down on the living room couch.

"Barely. At least my snowman was better."

"It didn't have any eyes or arms. It was horrible," Aspynn said teasing her brother.

"Shut up," he responded, laughing.

"Kids, want some hot cocoa?" the twins' grandmother asked.

"Yeah, sure," they both said simultaneously.

"Thanks Grandma," they again said simultaneously.

"So what do you wanna do now? We've spent hours outside and it's too cold to go out again," Steven said to his sister.

"Want to play the Nintendo 64?"

"Super Smash Bros?"

"Yep."

"Thanks Grandma," they said, while their grandma sat two mugs on the coffee table in front of the couch.

"You're welcome," she said walking away back to the den.

"Best out of three?" Steven said.

"Sure. Just don't get sad when I win."

"In your dreams."

* * *

"You only won because at the last minute Kirby fell off the tree," Steven said taking a sip of his hot cocoa.

"Yeah, sure, you just don't want to admit that you lost," Aspynn responded, also taking a sip of her hot cocoa."

"You know today was a good day after all, even though it's

not even over yet. I just wish we could have spent it with mom and dad," Steven said.

"Yeah. It was a good day, though. Just wish we had another snow day tomorrow."

"Yeah, and repeat this day all over again."

"Well, the day isn't over yet"

JANUARY 4

Olivia Figueroa
Age 13

The day was officially here. Alice was going to take her driver's test, so she could finally get the license she was waiting for. That was, of course, after she went to school. Alice started running down the stairs to the kitchen to eat breakfast. She glanced out of window and stopped herself. "What?" she said, confused. Outside, the ground was covered in blankets of snow. *This isn't good . . .* she thought to herself.

At breakfast, she sat staring at the little screen of her family's television, searching for the name of her school on the list of closed schools. Many minutes passed, and she saw nothing. Relief started to flood her, because she knew if school wasn't cancelled, then the roads would still be good enough for her to take her test. But then she saw it: at the very bottom of the screen was her school's name. She squinted and read: "Huron High School: CLOSED."

"Mom!" Alice yelled.

Her mom appeared in the kitchen. "Yes, darling?" her mom asked.

Alice took in a deep breath, "School is cancelled. Does this mean my test is cancelled also?"

Her mom frowned. "Yes. In fact, I just got a call from the place. They're closed for today," her mom paused, noticing the hurt look on Alice's face. "I'm sorry honey—I knew you were really looking forward to your driver's test."

"It's okay," Alice said, but both Alice and her mom knew she was upset. Leaving it at that, Alice stood up and left the kitchen, heading back to her room.

As she entered her room, she saw her older sister, Kara, standing near her mirror. "What are you doing in here!?" Alice demanded.

"Just looking for MY scarf that YOU took," Kara said with a smirk. Oh, how Alice disliked her sister. They could never get along. Stealing Alice's belongings was one of the many things her older sister did to pick on her.

Kara glanced at Alice's bed. "Hah!" she snorted. "I forgot that you collect Beanie Babies. Those things are so childish!"

Alice sighed. "Just get out."

Kara frowned and sashayed out of the room.

Despite the bad weather, Alice still wanted to go outside. She was upset that she couldn't take the test and wanted to let off some steam. She had to use her scooter because she didn't have her license to drive a car. Her mom and dad were both at work, and she certainly didn't feel like staying at home with her sister. "Even if the roads are bad," she thought to herself, "it's better to be out and about than to be cooped up with Kara."

As Alice rode on, she started to notice how cold it was outside. She pulled over, stopped her scooter, and searched through her bag for a scarf or a hat. As she got back on the scooter, she noticed that it wouldn't start. "Hmm, that's odd," she said to herself. She tried again, and once again, her scooter didn't start. She started to worry. *How was she going to get back home?* It would take her at least an hour to walk back, because of all the snow that was still falling from the sky. She didn't have a cell phone, as it wasn't common for people her age to have them, so she would have to walk to the nearest store or gas station to contact her sister.

When she finally reached a small gas station, she went up to the payphone outside. Luckily, she always carried around change with her in case a situation like this occurred. She dialed the only number she knew by heart. Kara picked up.

"Where have you been? You had me worried sick that you ran away. You never leave the house without telling anyone!"

"I know," Alice said, "I'm just upset that I didn't get the chance to take the test that I was really looking forward to."

Kara sighed. "Where exactly are you?"

Alice responded with, "The gas station just a few miles away from home."

"Alright, I'll be there soon," Kara said. Alice hung up.

Kara arrived, and the two of them drove home together. "Hey, I have an idea," said Kara.

"What is it?" asked Alice.

"Why don't we build a snowman? It'll give us something to do."

Alice was surprised. Her sister rarely wanted to do things with her. "Why not?" Alice grinned. And the two set off to find accessories for their soon-to-be snowman.

"Why don't we give it overalls?" suggested Alice.

Kara laughed, and added, "Or BIG sunglasses?" After about an hour, the two had finished their masterpiece.

"*Voila*!" shouted Alice. Kara picked up a snowball and threw it at Alice.

"Hey! That's not nice!" Alice said. But soon enough, Alice had picked up a snowball and had thrown it at Kara. Soon the two were in a full-fledged snowball fight.

After they had gotten tired, the two girls decided to go inside. Kara made delicious hot chocolate for both of the girls. "You know, I only pick on you 'cause I love you," said Kara.

Alice pondered what Kara had said. "I always thought you didn't like me," Alice said.

"No, I'm just your big sister. We don't ALWAYS have to get along," Kara said. After that, the girls played games like Jumanji, Monopoly, and Perfection for the rest of the afternoon.

Later that day, Alice's parents came home from work. "I have good news!" said her mom.

"What is it?" Alice asked.

"While I was at work, I called in to your driver's training facility, and I managed to get it moved to next Wednesday! So you'll get to take it pretty soon."

Alice rushed up to her mother and gave her a big hug. "Thanks Mom," she said.

Alice was happy. She started to enjoy being with her sister, and her driver's test was right around the corner. Alice thought to herself, *Maybe this day wasn't so bad after all.*

OCTOBER 14

Michael A. Zamborowski
Age 13

the darkness after the light

Ring ring clank clank. "Yes?" asked David groggily.

"Sir, it's Private Dawson and, well my wife just told your wife about Operation Allied Force," said Private Dawson.

"Oh crap," said David. "I gotta go man, thanks."

As David ran to the back door he heard his wife yell, "DAVID, YOU SAID YOU WERE TRAINING SOLDIERS AT FORT WAYNE!"

He was outside and was near the tracks. He walked slowly over to a long-haired man in jungle fatigues, smoking a cigarette. With a closer look at the man, he saw he had a Purple Heart around his neck.

FORT WAYNE, MICHIGAN
PFC DAVID SOBIESKI
0300 HOURS
JULY 30, 1990

"MOVE! MOVE! MOVE! COME ON, THIS AIN'T YOUR GRANDMA'S HOUSE!" yelled the drill sergeant. Moving quickly through the course, David saw the next obstacle.

"UNDER THE WIRE, THOSE ARE LIVE ROUNDS,

BOYS."

He made it to the last obstacle and got to the end to see General Horner.

"Come here, Private Sobieski," said General Horner. "Come to my office, Private."

"Sir, yes sir," said David.

As they walked to a door, the general looked back at David and said, "You have impressed the right people, son."

OCTOBER 14, 1999
BRIGHTON, MICHIGAN
DAVID SOBIESKI
0800 HOURS

"Hey boy, you alright?" asked the long-haired man.

"Yeah, I'm fine, just . . . I'm fine," answered David.

"I ain't seen anybody be out of it for that long since Nam," said the man. "Name's Jack, by the way. I didn't catch yours."

"Sobieski, David Sobieski," replied David.

"You happen to be related to a Paul Sobieski?" asked Jack.

"Yes, Paul is my father's name," said David, "but he has been missing for years."

"Sorry to tell you son, but your dad died in Nam from a Bouncing Betty," said Jack.

"Oh my God, Ma always told me he went to get a lotto ticket and never came back," said David. "Why would she lie to me like that?" David asked himself out loud.

"Listen, kid, I never met your mom, but your dad talked about her a lot, and he always said that she didn't want you joining the army like your old man," said Jack.

"Yeah, well that didn't work well, now did it?" said David under his breath.

"Well, like they say, like father like son," chuckled Jack.

"Not a hundred percent true—I was in the Air Force. Let's get out of the rain," said David

"Best idea I've heard all year," said Jack.

As they walked back to David's house they heard, "I Feel Good" by James Brown.

2001

JANUARY 28

Rami Emad Breadiy
Age 13

Harry Clare lived in Ann Arbor, Michigan. He was fourteen years old. It was January 28, 2001, the day of the Super Bowl. That was the year they had to move. Harry did not want to move because he was happy with his life in Ann Arbor, Michigan, and he had lots of friends. They had to move to Detroit, an hour away.

"*Mmm*," Harry said, smelling the fresh scent of chocolate pancakes. He went downstairs to eat breakfast and the news wasn't on, so he turned on the news. It said the weather was going be hot—73-83 degrees—today in Florida, and right then and there, his dad turned off the TV. He told Harry to go start packing up once he was done with breakfast.

"Okayyy," Harry said. He finished eating and went to his room to start packing up, and he turned on the TV. It said the Super Bowl today would be the best one yet. It was the Baltimore Ravens vs. New York Giants at Raymond James Stadium in Tampa, Florida. "Don't miss it," said the announcer. Harry said, "Cool" and he went downstairs and told his dad.

His dad said cool and he said that they could invite their friends over. Harry was happy and then he went to call his friends so they could come over. They said they could come over, so he went to set up some appetizers and popcorn.

Ding dong. Who was that? Harry ran to the door and saw his dad's friends Ian, Gabe, and Erik with the big New York

Giants symbol on their shirts.

How ugly is that? It makes me want to throw up, he thought. "Hi guys, come in."

Harry went to get his jersey on and his dad went to go put his New York Giants shirt on.

Harry said, "Well, I had gone to get my amazing purple Ravens jersey before your friends came," so he went upstairs and got ready. Harry said, "Dad, your friends are here." Jack, Bill, and Peter rang the doorbell.

"My friends are here, too," he said, as he went running down the stairs, and his dad followed. Harry opened the door and he saw his three friends, Ian, Gabe, and Erik, so he went with them to the family room and turned on the TV. The TV blared, "Hello everyone, we are in Tampa, Florida at the biggest Super Bowl yet, and with best two teams, the New York Giants vs. the Ravens."

"Wait Dad, I have an amazing idea," Harry said. "What if we make the biggest bet of all time? If we win, we stay here and don't move, but if you win, we move," he said.

His dad agreed and the pressure was on in first quarter, with the score at 7-0. In the second quarter, the score was 10-0. Harry said, "Hooray, we're winning in the third quarter with a 14-7 score!" There were more touchdowns in the fourth quarter and the game ended 34-7, with the Ravens winning! "Yes, we won, we won't have to move!" said Harry.

JUNE 28

Terrence A. Vick II
Age 13

Meet Brian. Brian was eighteen years old and lived in Detroit, Michigan. Brian was a very smart boy. He loved to play football and was very good. Everyone has a goal in life, and Brian had one. Even though his parents wanted him to play football, he liked to do music in his personal time as well. Brian was a percussionist in his school band, but his parents did not know. So how would he tell is loving parents what he wanted to do besides football? How would he tell his parents what his other passion was?

On June 28, he went to practice and he was quite discouraged. How was he going to tell his parents what else he wanted to do with his life besides football? As Brian was doing his normal routines to warm up for football practice, his coach noticed that he was a little depressed, so he pulled him to the side and tried to see what the problem was.

Meanwhile, his dad was waiting and waiting for him to come home from practice. Suddenly, Brian came home tired and sore, but not as depressingly sad as he was at practice. The room got silent and Brian's dad was waiting for him with his music and percussion sticks. Brian's father asked, "So, explain why I saw this in your room, Brian." Brian's heart started to pound very loud and hard. Brian already knew what his father was talking about . . .

* * *

While Brian and his father were having an argument, bordering on an altercation, Brian's father threw his sticks in the fire in the fireplace. Brian was very angry. Brian's mother came downstairs wondering what was going on between Brian and his father. Brian stormed out of the house and saw the pro football player Sage Taylor who played for the Detroit Lions as Number 27. Brian was mad and Sage wondered what was the matter with Brian. So Sage walked up to Brian and Sage started to talk to Brian. At first Brian didn't listen to Sage, but Sage started to talk to Brian about what he wanted to do in life, and what college he wanted to go to. Brian didn't discuss what he really wanted to do, but he listened anyway. So Sage started to talk about what things he did in football and Sage talked about the NFL and what he does in his training. Sage invited Brian to training facilities and Brian was very honored to be invited by pro football player Sage Taylor and to practice with him. Sage left and Brian kept walking to get his head in order, so he could be right and know what were the right things and respectful things to say to his parents. Brian came home, calmed down, and saw his parents. He apologized first to his mother and father for misbehaving and being disrespectful.

Later, he explained what he wanted to do besides football. His father opened up and let him fulfill his dreams to become a percussionist. Brian's parents talked to Brian and Brian told them what he wanted to do. Brian's dad realized that he had a life outside of football.

From then on, Brian's family supported Brian in everything he did and he started following his dream and became what he wanted to be.

AUGUST 24

Kiara Jones
Age 13

It was a summer morning day on August 24, 2001. Eva was warmly asleep until her friendly dog, Snuggles, jumped on Eva and gave her gentle kisses. Eva's mom called, "Eva, wake up! It's time for you to hurry over to Monica's."

"Mom, I just want to sleep," said Eva.

"No Eva, get up and get dressed," said Eva's mother.

"Fine, Mom," said Eva. Eva then got up. She hurried, grabbed her clothes, quickly put them on, and looked at her dad's army picture. "I miss you, Dad," said Eva. Eva let her dog out quickly and fed her saying, "You be good now, Snuggles—I'll be back in a while."

Eva started rushing out the door and rushed two houses down to Monica's house. Eva knocked on the door, but there was no reply. She took her extra key to Monica's house and opened the door.

"Hello?" said Eva.

Monica said, "Eva . . . you scared me!"

"Well, next time answer the door when I knock," Eva said, laughing. "Hurry and put on MTV so we can watch Aaliyah!" said Eva.

Monica quickly put on MTV and Aaliyah was on. Monica and Eva started dancing and singing while eating their breakfast. "I wish that I could meet Aaliyah! She's my role model!" said Eva. "She's such an inspiration to me. One day, I'm going to meet Aaliyah, and it's going to be the greatest day of my life," said Eva. Then, the Aaliyah music video "Try Again" came on. While Monica and Eva started dancing and singing, "If at first you don't succeed, then dust yourself off and try again."

Monica and Eva hurried to the bus stop and went to school.

After school, Eva and Monica came back home, saying, "See you tomorrow in the morning," again. Eva then rushed back home to her mom and her dog Snuggles. Snuggles started jumping on Eva with happiness that Eva was finally home. Eva's mom asked, "How was school, baby girl?"

"It was good" said Eva. Eva then suddenly started to cry.

"What's wrong, sweetheart?" said Eva's mother.

"I miss Dad . . . why did he have to go to the Marines? Why did he have to die? Why him? Why my dad? Didn't they know that he had a family to take care of?" said Eva while crying with such sadness.

"Because he had to fight for his country; he had to do what he had to do to keep our country safe . . . everyone who joins the army has a family. It's okay to be sad about that, Eva," said Eva's mother while wiping her tears. "Don't be too sad; tomorrow's your birthday."

"Okay Mom, night. I love you," said Eva.

"I love you too, sweetheart," said her mother.

August 25 , 2001 was a beautiful morning. Snuggles and Eva's mother jumped on Eva's bed. Eva's mother said, "HAPPY BIRTHDAY! You're finally fifteen years old!"

Eva woke up. "It's my birthday? Oh yeah, it is, hahahahaha, thank you, Mom," she said, while smiling ear to ear.

Eva's mom said, "I have a surprise for you." She was holding something behind her back. "What is it?" said Eva with such excitement.

"Tickets to Aaliyah's concert that she's going to have soon!" said Eva's mother.

"OMG! ARE YOU SERIOUS!? ARE YOU LYING!??!" said Eva with such shock. "I'm not kidding. See?" Eva's mom then showed Eva the tickets.

Eva hurried and rushed over to Monica's, knocking on the door quickly and loudly. Monica then answered, saying, "Happy birthday, Eva!"

"Thanks," said Eva, "but I have a surprise to tell you!" Eva then entered Monica's house saying, "Hurry and put MTV on, but that's not the surprise."

"Then what is it?" asked Monica with such caution and excitement.

"MY MOM GAVE ME TICKETS TO SEE AALIYAH IN CONCERT!!" said Eva, jumping around Monica's house.

"Are you serious?!" said Monica.

"Yes! These are the tickets!" Eva pulled out the tickets.

"OMG! WE'RE GONNA SEE AALIYAH!" they yelled, until they heard some shocking and sad news.

MTV announced, "Aaliyah has just died in a plane crash coming back from shooting the last parts of her music video 'Rock The Boat' in the Bahamas. This is a huge tragedy for the music industry and for Aaliyah's family and friends." Eva and Monica then started to cry.

"Are you serious? They have to be talking about a different Aaliyah; they can't be talking about her, they just can't! I don't believe them! This is not true!" said Eva as she cried, because her dreams of Aaliyah had been crushed.

Monica wiped the tears that fell down her cheek and grabbed their breakfast before they had school. "I'm sorry Eva, but it is true. Aaliyah is dead, but she'll be in a better place now," Monica said while gently patting Eva's back.

"It's not okay—my inspiration is gone now!" Eva said.

"There will be other inspirations as you continue life, Eva—you are not the only one who's sad. Everyone is sad about this, but she's going to be in a better place now. We have to go to school now," said Monica.

Eva then went to school. Everyone started to see a difference in Eva's behavior. Eva started to get horrible grades, she started to not talk to anyone, and started to isolate herself from everyone. She hardly ate her food or lunch at school. She didn't pay any attention to her dog Snuggles.

Eva's mother tried to talk to her, but Eva just didn't answer at all, until one day her mother went into the room and said, "Eva, this is ridiculous. You're getting horrible grades, isolating yourself, and you're not eating! Aaliyah was not a family member, she was just someone you looked up to. You have to move on and live your life."

"But it's for a reason. She died a few weeks after Dad died. That's two losses for me," said Eva.

"I understand Eva, but you have to live your life. Aaliyah and your dad will always be with you in your heart and you just have to remember that," said Eva's mom.

"Okay Mom, I'll try to remember that. Thank you for the advice. I'll get my stuff together," said Eva.

Years had passed and Eva had taken her mom's advice and kept her dad and Aaliyah in her heart and used them to motivate her through her life. Eva had worked hard at college at the University of Michigan and became a very successful doctor. If it wasn't for Eva's mother's advice, Eva wouldn't have continued so she could become a doctor. Eva is now living a wonderful life and makes sure all her patients are happy. Eva has never been happier.

SEPTEMBER 11

Ricardo Mojica
Age 13

He woke up at 4:58AM. *Beep beep beep!* His alarm went off. He was a little frightened by the noise, feeling destined to be someone and something that had to change. He was a little scared of what was waiting for him at 7:33AM in the Detroit Metro Airport. It was his first time traveling somewhere in an airplane. He had an athletics job interview in New York.

Later, he was on board the plane, but the pilot received a notice from the tower not to take off. There were signs of a terrorist attack on flights 11, 175, 77, and 93. The plane was not going to take off.

"Excuse me, ma'am," he asked.

"Yes?" replied the flight attendant.

"Why haven't we taken off?"

"Well sir, there is a risk that flights eleven, one seventy-five, seventy-seven, and ninety-three have been hijacked."

"Attention all passengers! The FAA's Boston center flight controllers have declared that flight eleven has been hijacked!"

The air marshall took his weapon out. "Everyone stay where you are!" he exclaimed. The police came on the flight and got everybody off. They announced, "All flights are cancelled until further notice."

"Why?" asked Ricardo.

"Because flight eleven has been hijacked!" yelled the police officer with suspicion in his voice. Ricardo was in shock.

Meanwhile, nineteen militants associated with the Islamic extremist group Al-qaeda hijacked four airlines and carried out an attack on the United States. In New York, people were scared because the planes were going to the Twin Towers. Two of the four planes destroyed the Twin Towers, another hit the Pentagon, and the last one was going to the White House, but due to the protesting passengers, the plane crashed in a Pennsylvania field instead.

The man was sad and angry at what had happened. 2,996 people died: 2,977 victims and nineteen hijackers. This was one of the worst tragedies that the country had witnessed. His job offer was postponed; he might have lost the chance to complete his dream to play for Real Madrid C.F. Later that week, the manager called and said, "You know what? We'll come to you!"

"Really?" replied Ricardo. "Yes, we could use someone like you on the team!" exclaimed Carlo Ancelotti.

SEPTEMBER 11

Michael Pocrnich
Age 13

"Love you, honey," Jerry's wife said. Jerry hugged his wife and she drove away. Jerry turned toward the door, got his plane ticket out, and walked inside. People everywhere. People rushing. People running, not walking, *running*. Business people, families everywhere. He walked toward the security: lines everywhere. As more people entered the airport, he became nervous that he was going to miss his flight. He stepped into the security line and waited. At least thirty people were ahead of him. He waited, people moved ahead, he moved again. He pulled out his watch. Twenty minutes left. This was going to be more than twenty minutes, at least. At this point he noticed a shorter line. He stepped into that line and it proved to be much quicker. He put his bags on the table.

As the security guard checked his bags, he interrogated Jerry. "Where are you going?"

"New York," Jerry responded.

"What for?"

"Oh, just to experience new stuff."

He looked up at Jerry. He handed him his bags. "Have a nice day."

Jerry went through security with no problem. Most of the people must have left. He took out his watch. Five minutes left.

He finally made it to the plane on time. He handed the

ticket to the lady.

"I am sorry sir, your plane has been delayed for two hours."

"For what reason?" Jerry asked.

"I am not allowed to say, sir. We will let you know when your plane is able to fly."

Confusion was the only thing that went through his head. "Huh, okay, thanks." Commotion filled the airport. People kept leaving, but Jerry was unable to figure out why. *Were there other planes being delayed for so long that people didn't even want to wait? Did others planes take off?* Vibrating in his pocket. He picked up his phone. He answered. It was his wife.

"JERRY, JERRY ARE YOU OKAY?" she cried in tears.

"Yeah, yeah, I'm fine, what's going on?"

"A plane has just crashed directly into one of the Twin Towers."

Jerry couldn't believe it. "Okay, yeah, my plane was delayed, I don't think I'm going. Can you come pick me up?" Jerry asked.

"Yeah, I'll come get you."

"Thanks. Bye." Jerry closed his phone and put it in his pocket.

He sat down and finally got a chance to observe his surroundings. The news was on everywhere. A report on CNN was announcing, "A plane has just crashed into one of the Twin Towers. This has just happened a few moments ago. We have very little information on this incident at this point in time, but we do have a report from someone who was near the incident. She said that she was on her way to work when she came out of the subway and saw a plane fly directly into the World Trade Center. We will bring you updates with more news of this incident as it happens."

Then the news showed a video of the crash. There was smoke everywhere coming from the top of the building. The smoke was so dark in the center. As it drifted away to the left it got lighter and lighter. You could hear emergency sirens everywhere. Jerry turned around. Everybody was scared, crying. Looking up at the TV. The same channel was on everywhere. Phones were ringing. More and more people were leaving the airport.

Jerry was shocked. He now knew that his trip to New York was not going to happen. Unsure of what to do next, Jerry picked up his stuff and went to sit on the curb, where his wife would pick him up. Traffic everywhere. Police sirens everywhere. All around the airport. You couldn't go anywhere without being stopped. Here she was. Scared, shocked, nervous, although relieved that he was safe. Jerry got into the car. They hugged and put Jerry's bags into the back of the car. Everything on the radio was about the situation in New York. If there was a song on, it ended ended shortly. It took hours to get home. Hours upon hours. Traffic everywhere you went. Jerry got home only to find a second plane crashed into the second Twin Tower and to find the first tower had collapsed. The second Twin Tower was about to collapse. The news showed pictures and videos of people jumping to their deaths. They said that another plane had crashed in Somerset County, Pennsylvania.

It only then came to Jerry that this was a terrorist attack, like what happened in Pearl Harbor. CNN said at 10:05 the second Twin Tower collapsed. Jerry couldn't believe it had happened. He only thought that this must be the last of it. Nothing could happen next. He wanted it to be over. The only possible site left was the White House. He was only hoping that this was over. Jerry got a phone call from his best friend Walt. Walt wanted to know if he had the news on. If Jerry was okay. Walt wanted to make sure that he wasn't in any type of danger. He wanted to come over. And sure he did. Walt and Jerry had been best friends since they were kids. They have been through everything together.

Knock knock. When Jerry opened the door, Walt said, "Hey buddy, how are you doing?"

"Good, good," Jerry said. "Hey, don't go back out there; traffic is bad out there."

Moments later, after staring at a TV, the last plane flew directly into the Pentagon. Jerry didn't know how to feel. He thought it was all over. He was only hoping that no one he knew was in one of those planes.

SEPTEMBER 11

Viola Cole
Age 13

Daniel and Emily had just gotten in the car when their mother gave them the news. They were going to New York on Tuesday. "I can't go to New York! I have a school fair this week! I really wanted to go! Please Mom, change your mind. Make it a different week!" Emily pleaded to her mother.

"Oh Emily! There are better things than a school fair. For instance, a real, public fair is way cooler!" Her mother tried to reason with her, but it was a hopeless case. Emily Carter would not agree to go to New York.

"Oh, come on, Ems! Grandma Bea lives in New York! I know you love Grandma Bea!" Daniel said.

Daniel hit Emily's soft spot; she finally said she would go. She did not want to go to school the next day. Her mom said all kids her age have to when they can, but there are plenty of kids who missed out on school because they were leaving the next day. Her brother was able to stay home and pack, but he was seventeen and she was only seven, well turning seven in February. She did not want to go to New York. It sounded like "ew pork," and she did not want to go to a place that sounded like "ew pork!"

Michigan was a lovely state; it was the shape of a hand with its beautiful lakes, how nice the summers were, and the snowy winters. It was the best! Her mother decided that she was going to have to convince her. She told her about how beautiful the buildings were and about the Statue of Liberty. She told her about the Twin Towers and how amazing they were when you looked up at them when the sun started setting. Emily closed her eyes and imagined this fantastic city her mother told her about, with buildings like the Empire State Building. Emily gazed at the air in awe, trying to imagine the beauty of this city. Maybe it wasn't so "ew pork" after all . . .

"Okay, I will go, but you have to promise me we are going to Times Square!" Emily demanded.

"I promise." Those were the last words she heard that night from her mother. Emily laid awake trying to imagine herself in New York. She imagined how many famous people would be in their fabulous clothes. She imagined the countless number of skyscrapers and the coast. Oh the coast—she imagined herself walking along the coast. She started to drift off to sleep as she imagined herself in some dashing clothes. She dreamt of herself by the Twin To-*BEEP BEEP BEEP!* Her dream was interrupted by the sound of her alarm. Not even two seconds after she shut off her alarm did Emily's mother come in.

"Good morning, sleepy head!" Emily's mother made it impossible for her to fall back asleep. She pulled the covers over head trying to ignore her, but her mother just yanked them off of her.

"MOM! I AM TOO TIRED FOR SCHOOL!" Emily tried to give a good reason to stay in bed; she even said her stomach started to hurt.

"Okay, go back to your silly dreams! But you are gonna miss out on the special suprise I have planned!" Her mother started to walk out the door.

"Wait! Mom . . . okay . . . " Emily shrugged out of bed.

"That's more like it!" Her mother smiled with success. Emily dragged her feet to the bathroom, slowly brushed her teeth, and took forever getting ready. She thumped down the steps and huffed and puffed to the table and plopped in her chair and never looked up while eating her food.

"Emily! Stop moping and hurry your butt up!" her mom yelled at her. Emily just glared through the thin strands of hair that fell down in front of her face. "Come on, let's go . . ." Emily wrapped her arms around herself; it was really windy this morning. When she got to school she told all of her friends that she was going to New York.

"Oh Emily! You are so lucky!! It's a shame I can't go with you," said her best friend in the whole wide world. Emily was still sad that she didn't get to go to the fair, but she did enjoy the extra cookies she got during lunch.

"I am going to New York tomorrow, too!" squealed a voice from the crowd of first graders, but that wasn't just any voice. That was Katie Evergreen. She was the sweetest, kindest girl ever. Also, she was the next best friend of Emily.

"Are you really?" Emily squeaked with her little voice, really excited.

"Yes! I am going because my dad has a business trip and Mommy suggested we with go with him so he wasn't so lonely," Katie shared with excitement. The rest of Emily's day went smoothly.

"Hey girl, come on, we gotta pack you some clothes!" Emily's mom said as she got in the car. Since Emily was only six, her mom just had to pick her up early so she never really got to stay after with her friends. They got home and Daniel was fast asleep on the couch with the TV on and a snack on the coffee table next to him.

"Daniel!" their mom said loudly enough to wake him, "Did you finish packing?"

"Yeah, I did," Daniel said with a tone.

"Okay, just making sure," his mom said with a *calm down* in her voice. "Emily, go on upstairs." Emily walked up the stairs and plopped down on her bed and started packing. She was excited that Katie was going too, and maybe if she was really good today, she could spend time with her in New York. So Emily stayed on her best behavior the rest of the day and later she told her mom that Katie was going.

"So Mom, since you seem to trust Katie's mom so much," Emily said with a sweet voice, "may I spend time with them in New York?"

Her mother looked at Emily and thought for a moment, "I was saving this for later, but while we are in New York we will be with Grandma Bea."

"Oh, so I can't?" Emily asked.

"Well, on our flight down she said she was gonna get you two something, but if you want, I can tell her you would rather be with Katie, okay?" her mother said.

"Okay, I guess I can stay with you guys..." Emily was not about to pass up a present from Grandma Bea. She decided it was more important to visit her Grandma than her friend. That night, Emily felt a rock in her throat and butterflies in her stomach. She was colder than usual and felt rather pale. With this achey feeling, Emily did not wait to fall asleep; she closed her eyes and curled up in a ball and passed out.

Then, instead of her alarm, Emily woke by the cold hand of her mother on her forehead. "Are you okay, sweetie?" said her mom with concern in her voice, "You look pale and you're very warm."

"My tummy hurts and so does my throat, but I am not warm—I am freezing," Emily said with a raspy voice.

"Oh honey, you are sick! I am gonna go tell Daniel, and then call the airport to get our tickets back, okay?" her mother said. Emily did want to go to New York now, and she didn't want to not go, so she replied, "Okay, but can you take us to New York later?"

"Yes," her mother said.

Emily and Daniel's mother was in the kitchen, whipping up some soup for Emily while on the phone with the airport trying to find out how to get their tickets either refunded or rescheduled. Emily was still curled up in her bed when Daniel walked to the opening of her door and tapped on the open door with his fist. "Hey Ems? On a scale of one to ten, how bad are you feeling?" he asked with a soft, calm voice.

"Seven, if ten is the worst," Emily said without moving.

"Okay, well, hope you feel better Emily." That was the first time that Emily could remember hearing her brother call her Emily. She rolled over and said thanks before her brother left. He turned at her and smiled, and went back downstairs.

Meanwhile, their mom was unpacking the car and telling Daniel's school that he was coming to school tomorrow. Emily's mom got the tickets rescheduled for September 25, giving Emily enough time to recover. Daniel was outside shooting hoops, while Emily was eating some soup watching Popeye and Betty Boop on the TV. Their mother was cleaning around the house and told her work that she needed extra time off because her daughter was sick, and that she would be leaving for New York on September 25. It wasn't even nine o'clock in the morning when Emily was flipping through the channels and past the news. "—are looking at obviously a very disturbing live shot there. That is the World Trade Center—"

Emily flipped the channel. "Wait! Go back!" Emily's mom said and looked at the TV. "—unconfirmed reports that a plane has crashed into one of the towers of the World Trade Center." Emily's mother gazed without blinking at the TV, with fear in her eyes. Emily looked back and forth at her mother and the TV, confused about what was happening.

When Daniel came in and looked at their mom, he said, "What's wrong?" while wiping the sweat off of his forehead. He looked in the direction his mother was facing, which was toward the TV and watched the news for a second.

"Right now, we are just beginning to work on this story, obviously calling our sources, trying to figure out what happened, but clearly something very devastating is happening this morning on the south end of the island of Manhattan.

That is, once again, a picture of one of the towers of the World Trade Center." Daniel and his mother stayed still staring at the TV. Emily sat there severely confused. "What? What did that mean?" Without answering her, Emily's mother grabbed the phone and started to call her mother. It went to voicemail and when it beeped their mom said, "Mom. It's me, Myka? Are you okay? Please tell me you left the Trade Center . . . " Their mother burst into tears and hung up the phone.

"Mom? What did you mean by *left the trade center?*" Daniel said with tears coming out.

"Daniel . . . oh Daniel!" His mom said running up and hugging him while crying on his shoulder.

"Mama, why did you call Grandma Bea?" Emily said with a sad voice.

"Because Emily," her mom said bending down to her, "Grandma Bea was at the big building on the TV. I just wanted to make sure she was okay . . ." Emily's mom started hugging her.

"Mama, is Grandma Bea okay?" Emily said hugging her back, starting to cry.

"I hope so . . . I really do . . ."

The family all sat on the floor hugging each other, crying, and hoping that their grandmother was okay.

The next day, someone came knocking at the door. Emily's mom came to the door and answered it. "Hello?"

"Good Morning. Are you Myka Carter?" the man, who looked like a police officer, said.

"Yes, what's this about?" Emily's mom said with concern in her voice.

"I come bearing bad news." The police officer stepped aside and a man who looked to be a lawyer came to the door.

"Myka, I am your mother's, Beatrice Bering's, lawyer. I have traveled all the way from New York. How do I say this? Your mother—she was in the Trade Center when the plane hit. I'm sure you heard of this?" said the man.

"Yes, is she alright? Are there any major injuries?" their mom said with hope in her voice that it wasn't what she thought. "Oh, no. No no no no."

"It is just that she was in a bad place at a bad time. She was . . . killed . . . in the crash."

Emily's mother's heart stopped. Her legs gave out and she became hard of breathing. Tears came running out of her eyes. Her stomach turned upside down and she seemed to just break down from the inside out. Emily's mother's heart gave up for a second and then she said, "And?"

The man and their mom were talking outside when the phone started ringing. Daniel was in the bathroom, so it was up to Emily to answer the phone. She picked up and said, "Hello?" in her mother's voice. "Hey Myka . . . " said a very sad voice. "It's me, Jaina. My sister Carla. Um . . . She was in the crash," Jaina sobbed. "I don't know what to do."

Emily clearly knew this person needed her mother even though she didn't understand. She told the person on the phone, "Um, I am sorry but I am Emily."

"Oh Emily! Is your mother home?" The woman on the phone sounded embarrassed.

"Um ye—"

"Who are you talking to?!?" interrupted her brother.

"A lady wants to talk to Mommy," Emily informed Daniel. "Okay, go outside and tell her. I will talk to the person on the phone," Daniel instructed Emily. She darted outside as if she was on an important mission and told her mom about the lady on the phone. Her mom told the lawyer to wait and ran inside to talk to the phone.

"Hello?" her mom said.

"Myka?" said the voice.

Emily's mom said, "Yes. What's wrong? You sound upset." The voice paused and then continued saying, "Carla was in the crash with—with her kids and Jack." Jaina started tearing up.

"Oh Jaina!" Emily's mom started tearing up to. "I am so sorry. Is there anything I can do?" The voice stopped and sounded like she was drying their tears. "Carla's daughter, Katie, had a dog."

"I can't! I am sorry but how can I—"

"Please Myka! Katie loved the dog so much! They are gonna send her to the pound! Katie would want Emily to care for her," the voice interrupted Emily's mom.

Emily was lying on the couch staring at the window, listening to their conversation, but could only understand her mom. "Mom, what happened?" Emily asked her mother with her raspy voice.

"Hold on, Emily." Her mother finished her conversation with the woman. "Fine, I'll take her. Emily will love it."

"Oh thank you! Thank you, thank you, thank you, thank you!" The voice was so loud and happy Emily could hear it. Her mother looked at her with depression. She then told Emily all about Grandma Bea and Katie Evergreen. Emily was very sad; she cried knowing that she would never see Katie or Grandma Bea again.

Then she was told about Katie's dog and how she was getting it. She loved and cared for the dog and named her Katie. Since the dog was only three, Emily got to keep her for a long time.

SEPTEMBER 18

Richarra Roach
Age 13

It had been a week since the World Trade Center went down. Jaden Marie Gorsonez was sitting on her couch in her small two-bedroom apartment, watching a news story about the planes crashing. She watched the story over and over again. She didn't know why she did it, she didn't know why she couldn't stop. She thought about her family living in New York and how horrifically close they stayed to the World Trade Center, or at least where they used to be, and how she's tried contacting them an endless amount of times, but still hasn't heard a single word from them. She couldn't take her mind off of how she couldn't get to them, or how helpless she felt to them. Most of all she thought about how all she's wanted for the past seven years was to be reunited with them, and now she may never see them again.

Jaden jumped up and rushed to her home phone when she heard it ring, hoping that it was one of her four family members in New York, but when she answered her phone she found that it was just the landlord telling her that she was late on the rent. With a heavy heart, she sighed and returned to her couch, only to continue to watching her news story.

As Jaden's thoughts drifted off into other areas of her mind, she began to remember that she had more things to worry about. Like the huge exam that she needed to pass coming up in her psychology class, even if psychology was just her minor. Or the piles of homework that she hadn't touched, and how her apartment looked like a pig pen due to the lack of chores. Oh yeah, and she was late on the rent, but in comparison to her family's safety, all of her other worries were nothing to be concerned with. It didn't matter, Jaden had somewhere to be. She got up, got dressed, grabbed a banana just to have something in her stomach for the afternoon, and walked out of the front door to go to work.

Jaden worked at Puffer Red's—the shoe store in downtown Ypsilanti. She also worked part-time as a waitress at Chili's, but her next shift there wasn't until Thursday. Today Puffer Red's was empty, as it should be; who would be concerned with getting new gym shoes in a time like this? Her shift didn't go by too slowly; however, her co-workers Trinton, Jayson, and Mia cheered her up like they always did. They made her smile and laugh and forget about all of her problems for a little while, and she was genuinely happy.

When Jaden's shift ended, she changed out of her work clothes into her casual day clothes—the Michigan Wolverines hoodie that she always wore, a pair of leggings, and her oldest, most comfortable pair of Jordans—then walked out of the front door to her car. When she got there, she just sat there for a while and let her mind take a break from all of the thoughts that were constantly running through her mind, and somewhere in the midst of that she dozed off and fell asleep. She dreamt of her idea of a perfect life. She dreamt of her family—the only people in the world she held close to her heart—she dreamt that they were all together again: her two cousins, her sister, and her grandfather, or PaPa as she called him. Everything was perfect and she'd never been happier.

Then something woke her up. It was Mia knocking on the car window. When she rolled it down, Mia asked her if she could come over and help her study for the psychology exam coming up, because Mia was in her psychology class too. Jaden agreed, because she hadn't studied at all either. She told her that she would be over her house at 8:00 that night. Mia's face lit up as she said "Okay, see you later," and walked away to her car. Jaden started her car up and drove home.

When Jaden got to her apartment door, she couldn't find her key which must have fallen off of her keychain, again. She dug through her work bag, and, of course, found them at the very bottom. She opened her apartment door and went in. She found that there was a message on her answering machine that wasn't from her landlord or from a phone in New York. This was strange to her, because there was nobody else who she thought would call. After thinking for a few seconds, she assumed that it was Mia calling to assure that Jaden was going over to her house tonight, but she never gave Mia her number. She was wondering and decided to just check her message, but when she did, she found that the message was from someone she would never expect.

"Hello? I'm looking for Jaden M. Gorsonez. My name is Alayzia Welsh. I've seen some of Jaden's work. I'm very interested and would like to speak with her, so if Ms. Gorsonez could call this number back when she gets the chance, it would be appreciated. Thank you for your time," the voice message said.

It was Alayzia Welsh! Not only one of the biggest names in the journalism business, but also Jaden's idol. She'd wanted to be just like her since she was twelve years old. She had heard her speak at a poetry night that her father took her to. Jaden couldn't believe what she was hearing; she thought she was dreaming.

When she called the number that Alayzia left, it went straight to her secretary's office: "Ms. Welsh's office, please hold." After being on hold for about fifteen minutes, Alayzia's secretary answered the phone.

"Hello? How may I help you?"

"Yes," Jaden replied, "I received a message from Ms. Welsh asking me to call this number. She said she was interested in my work and would like to speak with me. Is she available right now?"

"Why, yes she is. I'll transfer you to her right now, hun. Hold on."

After waiting for a few minutes, Alayzia answered the phone.

"Hello? Jaden Gorsonez?"

Jaden was in shock; she didn't know what to say.

"Hello? Is anybody there?"

"YES!" Jaden yelled out of panic. "This is Jaden M. Gorsonez. I'm a huge fan of your work, and I'm so honored that you're actually interested in mine."

"Oh, well thank you, sweetie. How about you come into my office tomorrow and we can talk."

"I'm sorry, Ms.Welch," Jaden said sadly, "but your office is all the way in New York, and I live in Michigan. There's no way I could afford to come in tomorrow. Is there any other way this could be done?"

"Hmm . . . well, I am going to be in Ann Arbor in two days; my kids and I go to that burger place, Blimpy's, every year. Do you think that there is any way you could meet me there?"

"Now that I can do. I'll see you in two days at Blimpy's, at say 2:30?"

"Sure thing, I'll see you then."

Jaden thought it was too good to be true. Her idol just called her and told her that she was interested in her work and now she was actually going to be meeting her in two days!

* * *

Jaden had to tell somebody, anybody, about what just happened to her. Jaden looked at the clock and saw that it was 7:00PM and she'd be right on time if she left for Mia's house that instant, so that's exactly what she did.

When Jaden got to Mia's house and Mia opened the door

to her apartment, Jaden instantly gave her a huge hug. Mia was confused, but she hugged back anyway. When Jaden let go of her, she asked what the hug was for. Jaden told her that one of the best things that could possibly happen to her, happened to her. She explained how Alayzia Welsh just called her and asked to meet with her in two days. Mia got excited too, as if the same thing was happening to her. She gave Jaden a huge congratulations hug, and then they began to study.

The next day Alayzia called back to confirm that they were meeting at Blimpy's the next day. Jaden told her that she looked forward to meeting her in person. Then a thought came to her that Alayzia may know her family. The chances were slim, but she had to ask. She asked Alayzia if she knew any of her family living in New York—Malia, Austin, Herbert, or Leo Gorsonez, and it turned out that she did! She knew all of them because they lived in the apartment next to hers, and said they were all always so nice. Jaden asked if maybe she could bring them in when they met tomorrow and she agreed to do it. Jaden's joy was overwhelming. Everything, every last thing that was happening was unbelievable.

Then Alayzia said, "I'm so sorry for your loss."

Jaden turned pale. "W-what do you mean?"

"Your cousin Austin—he didn't make it after the planes crashed."

Jaden's mind was spinning. She heard the words loud and clear but she still couldn't make sense of them. She hung up the phone and stood in disbelief. Once she came to her senses, she began to cry and she did so for a while, but once she stopped, she called Alayzia back and apologized for hanging up on her. She confirmed that they were meeting tomorrow at Blimpy's and that she would very much appreciate if she could bring in rest of her family with her. Alayzia agreed to it.

That next day they met up outside of Blimpy's. Jaden began to cry when she spotted Alayzia with her family, not because her cousin wasn't with them, but because she thought she lost all of her family, but she didn't. They were all there, practically right in front of her. As she watched them walk her way, she realized how unbelievably lucky she was to finally be reunited with her family again for the first time in seven years.

She couldn't wait any longer. She ran to her family and gave all three of them the biggest hug she could possibly give. And she was happy. And everything was perfect.

2005

JULY 9

Fatima Ali-Khodja
Age 13

"Daddy, can we get the Xbox 360 when it comes out?" April asked in her sweet little voice

"What for?" April's dad asked.

"It's going to be the best! You can play all kinds of games on it, and I really want it! Please!" April explained, as she leaned up to the front of the car so she could see both her parents' faces.

"But you don't need it," April's dad said.

"Well, we don't need a lot of things, but we have them," April said

"How much is it?" her dad asked.

"Three hundred dollars," she said.

"Absolutely not," her mother told her.

"Why not?" April asked. "It's not that expensive."

"It's not about the money. You just don't need it," her mother said. "Look, if you want it, you have to earn the money to buy it yourself."

"How am I supposed to do that?" April asked.

"Get a summer job," her mother told her.

"Ugh, this is so unfair," April groaned.

* * *

After three hours in the car, they finally reached their lake house. As soon as the car was parked, April jumped out and ran up into their house. She unpacked all of her things and, of course, put her one and only favorite elephant Webkinz on her bed. She missed being here and being here meant the beginning of summer break. Summer meant warm weather and no snow, it meant swimming, it meant hanging out with friends, and it meant she could finally start her driving lessons. April was so excited.

When April was done unpacking, she took her laptop out and searched summer jobs for fifteen-year-olds. Many different ads popped up. She narrowed down her choices to three different jobs. The first one was working for the veterinarian as a secretary and assistant, the second was being a waiter at a nearby diner, and the third was at the clothing store as a store clerk. April applied to all three, just to see what would happen.

April decided that she wanted to go down to the beach so she grabbed her favorite pair of giant sunglasses and a pair of flip flops. When she reached the beach she realized she didn't need flip flops. She loved the way the warm sand felt between her toes and the way when she walked closer to the water, it would wash up on the shore and touch her feet. April loved being up north.

April walked downstairs and out the front door only to find her mother and father sitting down at the picnic table with her little brother, who was playing with the sand.

"I have narrowed my job choices down to three," April announced.

"And what would those three choices be?" her mother asked.

"Either working for a veterinarian or as a store clerk or as a waiter," April said.

"I think the store clerk would be the best fit for you," her mother told her.

"Yeah, I think I like that one the best," April said, "but hey, if it earns me money, I want it!"

"Let's go swimming!" she told her brother.

They swam for hours.

As they were walking into their house, April said, "You know Alex, the lakes are the best part of Michigan."

"Agreed," Alex said. "Tomorrow we should go boating."

"Yes!" April said, excited.

The next morning, she woke up to find an email on her computer. She opened the email and it stated that the diner wanted an interview on Friday, July 8, 2005. April was excited, but a little disappointed that she didn't get an interview from the clothing store.

Then three days later, her best friend Abby met them up north. She had a house right next to April's on the lake. Their families were very close; they did a lot together. When they went to Mackinac Island, the first thing Abby and April did was go shopping. They both loved shopping. They walked into an accessories store.

"Do you like these?" Abby asked April, putting on a big pair of bright blue sunglasses.

"Yes," April answered, "they remind me of the color of the lake."

"Yeah, I love the color too," Abby said.

"You should get them," April said.

"OMG! I need this!" Abby squealed as she picked up a small penguin Webkinz.

"It's so cute! I think that I will get it for my little sister."

"Do you really think Jenna needs another stuffed animal?" April asked.

"Probably not, but I know she'll love it," Abby said

"Do you think this shirt is cute?"

"Sorry, but try this," April said, "it's way cuter."

They paid and left.

When April arrived home, she found two emails waiting for her. One stated that the veterinarian spot had been filled and that they were sorry. April wasn't that disappointed. She opened the next one; it stated that the clothing store wanted an interview on Monday, July 10, 2005. April was so excited that she started jumping up and down.

On July 8, April was so nervous. She dressed in what she thought was professional, which was tight black skinny jeans, flats, and a crop top. Big mistake. When she walked in, she was greeted by the hostess.

"I am here for the job interview," April said.

"You're April?" the hostess asked, looking at what April was wearing.

"Yes, I am," April said.

"Follow me."

The hostess took her to a table where a woman who looked about in her thirties was wearing glasses and reading a packet of paper.

"Hi, my name is April, and I am here for the job interview," April said.

"Oh, yoouuuu'rrre April," the woman said. "My name is Cindy, and I own and run this place." She stuck out her hand to shake. April took her hand to shake it, but it was like holding spaghetti. April just lightly shook it and let go.

"Why do you want to work here?" Cindy asked.

"Well, I would like to have a summer job so that I can earn some spending money and I think it could be fun," April explained.

"Huh, well I can tell you one thing: work is not fun and never will be," Cindy said.

"Um, okay . . . " April said a little stunned.

"So, how old are you, hun?" Cindy asked.

"Fifteen," April replied.

"Oh, well that's too bad," Cindy made a face and stood up, "Well then, I can't hire you here."

She started to walk away. "Why, why can't you hire me?" April asked.

Cindy kept walking and turned the corner to a long hallway and into an office.

"Wow," April said aloud.

April walked back up to the hostess that was writing on a notepad.

"Why can't she hire me?" April asked, "Is it because I am fifteen?"

"Oh hun, sorry if no one told you or if it's not on our website, but you have to be sixteen years old or older," the hostess said, "Sorry–safety reasons."

"Oh okay, thanks for telling me," April said.

April had started to walk out of the diner when the hostess said, "Also, next time, dress better."

April was sort of offended, but she could kind of understand why; she hadn't thought through her outfit.

April walked home a bit disappointed, but also a bit excited— now she could try dress better for her next interview. When she got home, she told her parents how the lady was kind of rude and that if she got the job, she wouldn't really want to work there. She told them how she got an interview for the clothing store and that she thought that would be better than working at the diner.

When April woke up on Monday, she was so excited for the job interview. She had planned out her outfit and it was much better than what she wore to the last one. April decided on wearing tight black jeans, a maroon shirt, a black blazer, and a silver necklace. April walked down the street and into the little town. She found the clothing store and walked in. She was greeted by a woman with a friendly face.

"Hello hun, can I help you with anything?" the woman with the kind face asked.

"Uh, yes, I am April. I am here for the job interview," April said.

"Oh, you're the young lady who applied," the woman said.

"Yes, I am." April stuck her hand out to shake the woman's hand.

"Oh, how very professional," the woman said shaking April's hand. "My name is Charlotte."

"Nice to meet you, Charlotte," April said, "I am fifteen years old. Will that be a problem?"

"Oh, not at all, I saw your résumé. If you were too young, I don't think I would have called you in for an interview," Charlotte said.

"Oh, okay."

They talked for about an hour. When she got home, she walked into the living room where her mother and father and two brothers were sitting watching TV.

"I got the job!" April announced. "She loved me."

"Oh that's great, honey," her mother said, "When do you start?"

"Next week, Monday," April told her mother.

When Monday came, April walked into the store to start her first day of work.

"Good morning, Charlotte!" April said.

"Morning, April sweetie," Charlotte said.

"What do I start with?" April asked.

"You can start by dressing the mannequins," Charlotte said.

April started dressing the mannequins. She loved being able to decide what the mannequins wore. When April got home, she told her parents that her day at work was the best. As she went to bed, April was excited for her day of work tomorrow. It didn't feel like work to April; it was just fun. April felt like she would enjoy working there and that it wouldn't just be work over the summer; it was going to be fun. She was glad that her mother told her to get a job, because it would get her the experience she wanted and needed for her future.

JULY 12

Sofie Gelderloos
Age 13

It was a regular, warm summer day in Saline. Isabella Adir was eating her routine breakfast of Honey Nut Cheerios. Isabella was a very independent fifteen-year-old. She had her own routine. She did chores without being asked, unlike her little brothers. She took care of herself. She already had her own job at the local Dairy Queen, and she was saving money for a trip. It was her dream to go to her mother's home country, Israel. She had predicted that by July, she would have saved enough to go.

It was July 12 at 2:00AM, and Isabella was already up and running. She was on her computer printing out her plane ticket. Her flight planned to arrive in Netanya, Israel at 6:30PM. She was supposed to take off at 5:30AM. She couldn't wait to visit her Aunt Adina. She loved her aunt so much. While she was packing, her mom came in and said,

"Guess who is coming with you? Me!"

"Yay," Isabella said, sarcastically.

"Oh c'mon, she is my sister, I would love to see her," her mother replied.

"Fine," sighed Isabella.

At 4:30, they left for the airport. They went through security and were boarding the plane by 5:20. It was about 5:40, and the plane still hadn't left. Isabella began to worry.

"Mom, what's going on?" Isabella asked in a shaky voice.

"I don't know. I will ask the flight attendant," her mom replied.

"Umm, excuse me, ma'am, why haven't we taken off yet?" her mother asked the flight attendant.

"There was an accident in the city where the plane is supposed to land. I don't know if we will be able to take off," the flight attendant replied.

Now Isabella was really upset. She was worried, sad, and disappointed. She wondered what had happened. She wondered if she would ever see her aunt again, if she would ever fulfill her dream of visiting her mother's home country.

"Mom, what if something happened to Aunt Adina?" she whispered to her mother.

"I'm sure she is fine—don't worry," her mother replied in a comforting voice.

She nodded trying not to show her increasing worry and disappointment.

Then the captain made an announcement,

"Sorry to say, ladies and gentleman, but we will not be leaving for Netanya, Israel today due to a serious accident at a mall. Again I am very sorry, and we hope you get on our next flight to Netanya, Israel on August the third."

"August third?" Isabella yelled. She began to cry.

"It's okay, Isabella," her mother said.

"We will just go then. I will call Aunt Adina right now," her mother continued.

The phone rang and rang. No one answered. "I will try again when we get inside," her mother said. When they were getting off of the plane, Isabella overheard the captain talking to a flight attendant.

"I can't believe people do such things, killing innocent people, and killing themselves," the captain said.

"That is the purpose of a suicide bombing," the flight attendant replied.

"Do you know how many people died?" the captain asked.

"Five dead and over ninety injured," the flight attendant answered.

"Do they know who they were?" the captain continued

"Yeah, it wa—"

Before Isabella could hear anymore, her mother grabbed her arm.

"C'mon sweetie," she said.

Once they got into the airport, they went to a cafe. Her mother tried to call Aunt Adina again. This time someone answered. Isabella saw her mother's face light up and then slowly turn to despair. When her mother hung up, Isabella had a million questions, but all she could say was, "Is she dead?"

"What?!" her mother replied, shocked.

"She died in the mall, didn't she?" Isabella began tearing up.

"Mom! Tell me if she is dead!" Isabella demanded. She was crying now.

"She was at the mall, buying gifts, when . . . " her mother began.

"When a guy blew himself and the people around him up, including Aunt Adina," Isabella interrupted, finishing her sentence.

"Let's go home," her mother said, fighting back her tears. Isabella hugged her mother and nodded, her eyes filled with tears.

When they got back, she laid in her bed saying goodbye, to Aunt Adina and her dream. With tears streaming down her face she whispered, "Goodbye."

AUGUST 20

Ethan Lichtenberg
Age 13

It was steamy outside. No, it was downright blazing. No sense in doing anything outside anyway. She already had cut the lawn yesterday. Also she has been too busy thinking about how to get herself a Facebook page. This is Katlyn Middleton; she lives in Ann Arbor on Munger Road with her brother, mom, and dad. She goes to Huron High School, but school isn't in session right now because it's summer. It's around 9:00 and she just got off the phone from talking to her friend about hanging out sometime soon.

"Hey Dad!" she yelled.

"What do you need, sweetie?" he replied

"Can you drive me to John's house?" she asked.

"Sure, around what time?" he asked.

"In a few minutes, Dad," she replied.

"Okay dear, you'll have to walk home though, or ask for a ride, because I'm going to work," he responded.

* * *

"Hey, John!" she greeted her friend.

"Aye, it's Katlyn!" he excitedly responded.

"Can't wait to get my driver's license, so no more being chauffeured everywhere by my dad," she complained

"So, you said you wanted to talk," he responded.

"Yeah, I wanted to talk to you about getting a Facebook

page because you are the hacker type," she informed him.

"I guess I could try to get you a dot edu email, but it will be difficult," he replied.

"If you could, I would hug you!" she giddily responded.

"I'll take you up on that!" he jokingly replied.

"Okay, let's go play some *Mario Party*!" she said. And they left to go play some Mario Party.

* * *

She was walking home in the blazing heat. She felt like she was dying and was very glad that she was wearing antiperspirant. *Dad did say that his work was getting Facebook, so maybe he can pull a few strings for me.*

"I'm home," she announced,

"Hi Katlyn," her brother replied.

"Why aren't you at Jacob's house, Michael?" she complained.

"Because Jacob is busy," he snootily responded.

"I'm home!" her dad announced.

"Back already, Dad?" she asked.

"Yeah, all we did was set up Facebook accounts," he replied.

"Really, could I get one, too?" she excitedly asked. Her heart raced as she watched her dad consider the options. *I could be the first kid in Huron High School to have one. Think of all the street cred I could get—Katlyn Middleton the first kid to have a Facebook . . .* All of this rushed through her head.

"No," her dad calmly replied.

"Bu-bu-but why?" she stuttered.

"Oh, and tell John that he doesn't have to hack you one either," he sternly replied.

Ring ring . . . ring ring . . .

"Go answer it," her dad said.

"Hello, who is it?" she asked.

"Hey! It's me John, don't shoot," he laughingly replied.

"Hey, I just talked to my dad and he said that I couldn't have a Facebook," she sadly replied.

"Dream crushed! So I guess I won't get one for you," he said.

"Yeah, I guess so," she said, and they hung up.

"So Dad, why can't I have a Facebook?" she asked

"Because no one else that you know will have one and everyone you'll end up talking to will be a grown man or a college student, that's why," her dad sternly replied.

"Guess that you're right . . . so no Facebook for me," she mumbled.

September 6, 2005

The first day of school was horrible. Everyone was asking her about her new Facebook and teasing her that she had failed at her biggest goal of the summer. The day went by slowly and it felt like it was going to take eternity to get out.

RING RING!

Yes, school was out! As she got on the bus, she felt like a weight had been lifted off her shoulders

* * *

"Hey honey!" her dad called

"Yeah, Dad?" she replied

"So, at my work today, they were talking about releasing Facebook to high schoolers, and I suggested that you could be one of the subjects. The kids would be from around the U.S. but they have to have a certain grade requirement, and I think I'd feel better if you got a Facebook now," he explained

" . . . and so would I, sweetie," her mom chimed in.

AUGUST 22

Jafiah Edwards
Age 14

"Let's go, Noah," Jacob called out to his little brother.

"Ten more minutes," Noah yelled from the basketball court.

"No, now! Mom and Dad are leaving soon," Jacob demanded.

Jacob was picking up his ten-year-old brother from school.

"Alright fine," Noah snapped.

"Hey, see you guys tomorrow," Noah said to his friends. On their way back, Jacob listened to his brother yap on about what he thought was wrong with the world and his life as they walked the streets of Detroit. Jacob used to have the same thoughts, however, they were on a much larger scale. But, he decided a long time ago that those thoughts wouldn't change anything. They wouldn't change where he lived or what he had to do to survive. Although, he was luckier than most. At least he had both his parents and his family had a decent amount of money. Because of his parents' money, they had saved and planned to go to New Orleans for their anniversary. They left today, August 22.

Jacob and Noah walked up the steps to their two story house. It wasn't a house someone would call healthy to live in. Dirty plates and bowls covered the stained counters, and although dust covered every crack in every corner, it was home to the Matthews family. As Jacob walked over the old wood floorboards to the kitchen, his father whizzed by.

"What's up, Dad?" asked Jacob.

"Just checking if I got everything! Cab should be here any moment," Dave answered. Just then a cab pulled up outside.

"Well, look at that." Dave said, "I must be psychic."

"Let's go Kyra, cab's here!" Dave yelled to his wife.

"Coming!" answered Kyra in a frantic voice.

Suddenly, Kyra came bounding down the stairs in a not so graceful way. Kyra was a short woman with a lot of spunk. She wore big loop earrings and loads of makeup on her face. Jacob and Noah waited by the door to say their goodbyes. Dave and Kyra hugged their boys.

"Love you guys. We'll be back in ten days, and remember, Noah, you must listen to Jacob. He is in charge," Kyra demanded.

"Yes, what she said," Dave added. Noah smirked. Dave and Kyra picked up their bags and headed to the cab. Once inside, they waved back to Jacob and Noah on the porch and said their last goodbyes.

"Remember, Noah, I'm in charge," Jacob reminded him.

"No way," Noah replied as he punched Jacob in the stomach.

The next day was quite difficult for Jacob because Noah listened to nothing Jacob had to say. Noah always left to play basketball with his friends. It did feel strange to Noah and Jacob not coming home after school to their parents. The food was supposed to last until they got back, but Noah scarfed it down like it was his last meal. This forced Jacob to go the corner store. Since his parents were gone, Jacob became more aware of what they did for Jacob and Noah. One night, Jacob sat on the futon with Noah as he called their parents in New Orleans. He was expecting an, "Oh my gosh, how are you boys? We miss you so much here!" but instead, no one answered. He called again, but still no answer.

"We'll call them tomorrow, Noah, they're probably busy," Jacob said.

"Man, I don't need them, I'm all grown up," Noah replied in a cocky voice.

"You need them more than you think, little boy," Jacob said.

"Don't call me that, Jacob!" Noah shouted as he tackled him.

As Jacob and Noah tread on through the days, they became worried about their parents. It had been three days since they left. Jacob and Noah sat on the futon every night and called them. But still they got no answer. Over these days, Jacob had become increasingly aware of Noah.

Each day, he seemed to grow sadder and his face drooped lower. Jacob actually missed the energetic little boy who would attack him with punches.

"It'll be alright," Jacob told Noah after every unanswered phone call.

* * *

On the fifth day of without contact with their parents, a man arrived at their house. Noah sprinted to the door in hope that it was his parents because they never got visitors. The sadness grew in him when he realized it wasn't them. He just turned from the door and walked away without opening it. Soon after, Jacob came, answered the door, and greeted the man.

"What is it?" asked Jacob. Jacob realized that the man looked unusually sad.

"Are you Jacob Matthews?" the man asked.

"Yes," replied Jacob. "What is it?"

"It's just that, I come bearing unpleasant news. There has been a terrible disaster in New Orleans and . . ."

When Jacob heard this, he felt like his spine was unhinging. Jacob dreaded what the man might say next.

"And there was a hurricane and . . . I'm terribly sorry," the man said sorrowfully. Jacob just stared at the man. He felt his eyes fill with tears and all the energy leave his body. He heard a yelp as he collapsed to his knees. He turned and saw Noah with terror-filled eyes looking at the man. Noah wanted to attack the man, but he was too weak to move. Jacob made his way over to Noah on his knees and embraced him. They held each other. As the man, he looked at the damage he had just created. The damage of two brothers, now parentless. It was the type of damage that could not be fixed.

AUGUST 28

Ari Barajas
Age 13

He called and called, but no one would answer. Most of them made an assumption that she was affected by the hurricane critically. Ryan didn't want to go in that state of mind, yet. He wasn't ready to accept that she might have died in the disaster. He wanted to forget about it. He knew that she was fine. He was hoping that maybe after the hurricane, she would find a way to contact them and say how sorry she was for not doing so sooner. Or maybe she had died. He wasn't sure what to think.

"Did she call at all?" He felt it was a stupid question to ask because he'd already known the answer.

"Not today. Do you still think she is out there?"

No, he thought.

"I do, do you?"

He didn't answer, of course.

"I just want you to know that if she isn't okay, we're going to be okay."

Ryan didn't really feel like hearing that.

He smiled and walked toward his room.

Ryan turned the TV on, just to get things off his mind.

Almost every channel was talking about the hurricane. He turned the TV off and just sat on his bed listening to music. A few thoughts ran through his mind. One led to another and soon he was thinking about his mom. Ryan hadn't seen her in almost two months. He came to visit his father, because he lived here in Michigan.

Ryan's father and mother had been divorced for five years. Ryan was seven when he heard the news. At only seven, he didn't quite understand why they couldn't make up like they always did. He remembered fights almost every day—screaming and yelling about money. Ryan didn't have a very good appraisal of things. Things were better now, though.

Both of his parents were remarried. Ryan's stepfather and mother had his little sister; she was so beautiful. Emma had a large heart and was very outgoing. She was full of life, wherever and whenever.

His father and his stepmother didn't have any children, but he thought that was better, because he got some attention. Although, Linda might have been sterile. Ryan heard a couple of conversations between them about a month ago. He heard that she was going through a pretty hard time. She begged him not to say anything.

Linda was such a great stepmother; she was always making lunch and jokes. She seemed happy ninety percent of the time. She became best friends with his mother. Both of them were like high school girls when they're together. Both of his families were very welcoming and full of love. *I miss my mother and Emma*, thought Ryan.

August 29, 2005

Ryan decided to take in more information about the disaster.

He felt the urge to watch the news. Maybe he felt like it would help to find his mom or something. He sat under the covers to prepare himself and whispered, "I honestly don't know why I'm nervous."

He turned the on the TV reluctantly and changed the

channel to CNN news.

"1,800 are reported dead and 6,600 are reported missing."

How likely was it for his mom to be one of them? The thought scared him.

There were houses and roads underwater.

If something wasn't underwater, it would be destroyed by the strong winds. Buildings were torn apart and cars were floating and sinking in the water. He felt a rush of gratitude that he wasn't there, then anger that his mother and Emma were there.

"Eighty percent of New Orleans is underwater," the news informed him.

Not only was Ryan worried about his own family, but also all the people who would end up homeless because of the traumatic disaster.

There were buses, cars, and trucks on top of houses. Trees had fallen down. Houses once considered homes had turned into scraps of trash.

Ryan shed a tear. He didn't know whether he would see his mother and Emma again. He was losing his remaining hope. He tried to convince himself that they were okay and that they had found shelter. He thought of all the good things that could've happened.

Even if he thought of only three, he would only hang on to those.

NOVEMBER 18

Odia Kaba
Age 13

The roads were pretty icy. Snow kept falling. It didn't look like it would stop any time soon. No matter how dangerous driving would be, Spencer wasn't canceling her plans. She had been planning this trip for weeks. Today, *Harry Potter and the Goblet of Fire* was coming out. She basically lived in the middle of nowhere. Muskegon was nothing but open land. There was a beautiful beach, but it was too cold to swim in, so there really wasn't much to do. In order to see Harry Potter, she had to drive for an hour to get to the cinema. Considering the conditions, she didn't think her mother would even let her out of the house.

"Spencer. I don't know. The roads are looking pretty bad."

"Ma, remember when I asked you earlier this month? You said it was alright to go. It's too late to change your mind. I've been saving up weeks now for today. We can't just let the money go to waste."

"Fine. But I have to drive you. It's too dangerous for a sixteen-year-old to drive by herself in this type of weather."

"I'm okay with that."

She decided that the album *Songs About Jane* would make the drive more interesting, along with Planters Cheez Balls and a can of Sprite Remix.

Her coat was a little tight; her mittens didn't cover all of her hands. It was not easy for her mom to afford new clothes.

She learned a long time ago to live with what she had. That meant that she would have to risk frostbite.

Stepping outside, she felt a blast of cold air. Her face was wet from the thick sheets of snow falling. The parts of her skin that were not covered started to feel numb.

Inside the car was just as cold. Ma turned on the heater as soon as the car was on.

Their old car took a while to warm up. When it finally did, they were relieved.

The main road was pretty crowded. They were not used to seeing it like that. The way to the highway was a very bumpy ride. Usually, they would say that the highway was safe because of how smooth it was, but this day was different. It was really crowded and slippery. Nobody seemed to have any control over their cars. They had already seen a couple of swerves. Spencer was feeling very uneasy. She looked over at Ma and her face said the same thing.

Maybe this wasn't a good idea after all. Guilt filled her stomach. She started to apologize to Ma, but before she could even open her mouth, she got a weird feeling. Everything was happening so fast. She felt like she was floating. She hit her head hard. She tasted blood. She heard shattering. She landed on her back. Before she could even register the pain, everything went numb. She couldn't feel anything. Everything went mute. All she could see was blackness.

2008

SEPTEMBER 3

Anthony Van
Age 13

Not a day went by without Thomas Pizza thinking about swimming. He woke up in his Ann Arbor suburban home, knowing that his possibility of becoming an Olympic swimmer had vanished. Recently, he had a leg injury due to jumping from a rooftop because he was peer pressured into doing it.

The smell of his favorite dish, pizza with bacon, pepperoni, and cheese, woke him up in the morning. He climbed down the staircase in his home, into the kitchen. Without thinking about brushing his teeth first, he dove into the pizza. Thomas's dad turned on the flat screen television and changed the channels to the sports channel. The channel showed replays of the Olympics. He saw that an Olympic swimming competition was about to start. Thomas got excited and his favorite swimmer, Michael Phelps, was getting ready. He saw his role model starting to swim. Thomas started feeling inspired to swim, but he thought about the grim and sad reality that he couldn't swim anymore.

He visited his community pool after breakfast. He used to go there almost every day to practice swimming. Now he couldn't go because of his injury. It saddened him greatly. He heard spashing, kids laughing and giggling, and it made him want to go and practice swimming.

His goal of becoming an Olympic swimmer faded away

as he heard the clear sounds of the pool. He got more depressed as he listened. He walked back home on his crutches. He tripped and felt sadder than before.

After he watched some more Olympic swimming competitions, Thomas wasn't sure if he should be feeling sad or inspired. His brother, Joe, entered his room and said, "The doctor sent a check-up report home!" Joe handed the doctor's report to Thomas. Thomas felt a little enlivened when he saw the paper. The report read, "You're okay now. You no longer need your crutches, but be cautious!"

Then after a while, Joe had another folded piece of paper in his hand, so Thomas reached for it. Joe resisted letting him grab it, but Thomas managed to take the folded paper. When he unfolded the paper, he saw a picture of Michael Phelps, and it was signed, "To Thomas Pizza, I hope your legs get better and that you become an Olympic swimmer, just like me! Your star, Michael Phelps." Thomas was very surprised. *Who could have told Michael about Thomas?* Thomas was feeling very excited by all these recent events. Then, Thomas looked at Joe and opened his mouth. Joe was the one that asked Michael to send him the letter.

Thomas decided to start practicing swimming. All the depression finally washed away. He put on his swim trunks and walked to the community pool. Thomas realized he didn't have a pass to get into the pool. The pool pass was unaffordable. Thomas did not have a lot of money. His parents and brother would most likely not lend him money because they were short on money. The pool owner decided to raise the entry price. He also couldn't enter the pool to practice because his legs didn't work well. He decided to just stop going to the pool. He thought that he could never swim again. Even the recent events couldn't help him. In the end, he felt like he couldn't even do anything anymore, even with his fixed legs. Thomas wasn't patient either, so that added to his minor depression.

Thomas thought, *What could he do?* He was sad and happy at the same time, since his legs were fine again. This was his thought process for the next few days. His brother, Joe, decided to help his little brother.

Joe started to help him with his devastated life. He bought him a pool pass. When Thomas discovered this, he was extremely delighted that he could go to the pool and practice to become an Olympic swimmer like Michael Phelps. This was an amazing turn of events. He decided to rush to the pool. Over the next few days, his legs recovered and he was able to swim too! Thomas was finally happy again. Months later, he was accepted into the Summer Youth Olympics for 2010. His model, Michael Phelps, still inspired him as he went.

NOVEMBER 3

James Cardwell
Age 13

"Wake up! Wake up, honey. Your breakfast is getting cold!" That's what Leonard Coldwell heard most of his mornings when he was under the custody of his mother. As Leonard was getting out of his bed, he had a shiver down his spine.

"Cold as usual," he said in a frustrated voice. "I'm coming, Mom!"

It was time to get ready for school and, besides, tomorrow was their day off, Election day. The floor was freezing and as soon as his bed covers came off, he was quick to get to his coat, which didn't seem to make much of a difference.

As Leonard was going down the stairs from his room, he saw his mom watching their old television.

"Just think of it, our country's first black president."

"But that's not all that matters when we are voting," Leonard's mom said.

He replied with a small grunt and walked into the kitchen. An omelet made with one egg and some leftover bacon and mushrooms.

"Well, it's better than when I get nothing," Leonard said. He took a bite and it was cold. As he ate his breakfast, he thought about it, about the thing he thinks about every day. *What should I do? How can I make money? Am I ever going to get out of this hell hole?*

Leonard finished his breakfast and got ready quickly.

November 3, 2008

As he walked out the door, his mom was watching the news. "Bigfoot report soon to be discovered as a hoax!" Leonard thought to himself, *Why should people make a big deal about that crap when people here are starving and living on the streets?* Then he shut the door with a slam.

The air was cold—so cold that Leonard could see his breath in the wind. As he walked down the street, he made deep tracks in the snow. "Oh that's right, it's snowing," Leonard said as he walked down the street to his bus stop. It wasn't really a pleasant sight though: empty bottles, cigarettes, even high piles of old trash. There were some pleasant sights though: kids getting up early to play in the snow, laughing.

As Leonard was waiting at his stop, he saw many people walking around or driving by with the new iPhones, wearing their geeky glasses, talking about politics and all the cool new apps on their phones. This annoyed him to the point where he kicked at the pole of a stop sign. The bus arrived and it was time to go to school.

Ring ting ring. That was the old rusted bell that Leonard heard every morning before school, telling him it was time for boring lectures by teachers who didn't even have the right education to teach. Leonard wasn't a very successful or accomplished student, but he was trying to learn and do the best as he could in class. *Soon, soon it will pay off*, he thought. His mother wasn't very educated and didn't finish college, so learning the material at school was all he could do—no second chances. It was his first hour of the day and it was already starting out badly. Kids were yelling, being obnoxious, and he was not even learning anything in the process.

"Well, six more hours to go," Leonard said.

In transition to his other class, Leonard was stopped by a kid. His name was Carver and he was known for being one of the more troubled kids. Carver approached Leonard. "Hey Leonard!" he said in an ugly, raspy voice.

"How's it goin'?" Leonard said, in an attempt to seem casual.

"Oh, well, I was just getting pretty hungry and thought I would collect some money from my best friend, you know?"

"And what if I say NO?" replied Leonard.

"Well . . . " At that point, more of his friends came out from behind the lockers and the sides of the hall. Then his shoulders were grabbed and the first punch came and hit him right in the gut. The next was in the corner of his eye and everything turned black.

Leonard woke up at home with an ice pack. His mother seemed upset. Then Leonard heard the voice of another women in the room. "I'm sorry Miss Parkins, but you don't have insurance; you can't afford the medical bill." Then his mother started crying. Leonard's eyes began to close and then he fell asleep.

"Good morning, again." Leonard was back in his house again. It was the morning after and Leonard couldn't remember what happened. "Honey, do you remember who hurt you?" his mother asked.

That's right, Leonard thought. At that moment he felt a searing pain in his head; it was burning hot, and he felt like his hair was on fire. "Ahhhh!" Leonard yelled out. His mother told him to rest.

Leonard woke up later that day and thought, *It's time to do something*. He got out of his bed and got ready. He had a daring thought in his mind: *There is only one way that I can make enough money to survive*. He was about to commit a crime.

11:00PM—that was the time Leonard chose to get out. But there was one problem . . . Leonard's mom slept downstairs. He slowly crept down in his black coat and gloves— *creak* went the stairs, as he was walking. Leonard went silent. Then continued until he got outside. He took a heavy breath and was on his way.

He arrived at his point of interest, Clare's Dry Cleaners.

He took out a crowbar that he had found in his house's storage and positioned it at the door. He thought to himself, *If there is an alarm, I need to be quick . . . it's time.* He broke open the door and then the alarm went off. *Bang* was the sound of his crowbar breaking through the metal cash register. His heart was pounding as he was loading the dollars into his bag. Sirens blared in the background; when he heard them he started to run. He he saw the lights in the distance. Now he was in a chase. Cops had their guns out. He started to run. As he took a shortcut into to an alleyway that he thought was there, he soon realized that it was blocked off, and he was stuck in a dead end.

"Put the weapon down!" the cop yelled. Leonard saw the end of his gun and tried to make a run for it. Then he heard a loud bang.

NOVEMBER 11

Derek Berger
Age 13

"Dad, I want an iPhone!" Andrew yelled from his room.

"Why do you need one? Besides, it came out a while ago!" his dad screamed back.

"Everyone at school has one besides me!"

"I'm sorry Andy, but it's not going to happen."

"Whatever." Andy mumbled. Andrew Jones, or just Andy, was a normal, but quirky young man. He loved to be in the know, but he was a little clumsy. He was fourteen years old and was in the eighth grade. Since the day the new iPhone with 3G came out, Andy dreamt about buying one—well, his parents buying him one. Yes, it was true that most kids in his school already had one, but Andy didn't. He was sick and tired of everyone going on the internet anytime they wanted to and playing games. As jealous as he was, his parents were very stubborn. All he wanted to do was fit in with everyone else and he thought having an iPhone would change all of that.

It was a normal Tuesday in November. Andy brushed his teeth, threw some clothes on, and bolted down the stairs to eat breakfast. He was running a little late because he spent some time having that depressing conversation about the phone with his dad. Andy gulped down a bowl of Cheerios and went to go grab his phone that was laying right where he left it by the charger. Before he unplugged his phone, he glanced next to it—there was his dad's iPhone, lying right next to it. Andrew had the urge to just take it for one day, but he knew his dad would find out. But then again, his dad worked from home . . . Andy stood there for a moment just wondering about the different outcomes that could possibly happen.

"You okay there, son?"

"Yeah," Andy quietly squeaked.

* * *

Andrew could see the lights of the bus flashing yellow and orange in the distance. A moment or two passed before the bus came to a stop. He took slow, large steps approaching the stairs that led to the darkness in the bus. He entered the bus like people enter a haunted house in those horror movies. Andrew Jones sat across from his friend in the back of the bus and whispered, "Look what I got!"

"What?" his friend whispered back. There, lying in Andy's hands, was his dad's cold iPhone. "You took your dad's phone!" screamed Andy's friend.

"Shhhhhhhhh!" Andy replied. "Don't be so loud, Colin, I don't want a lot of people to know. Besides, I'm only taking it for one day; I will give it back when I get home. He won't even notice that I took it."

"Wow, I can't believe you have the guts to take it. You better not lose it or else your dad will kill you."

"Yeah, yeah, I know. I'm not stupid. I just kind of . . . took it. I don't even remember putting my hand on the phone. It was like I was being controlled or something."

"Yeah, that's what happens when you want something really bad."

The bus ride went really fast and so did school. Andrew enjoyed showing all of his friends his "new phone" until it came to lunch. He went to the bathroom and left his dad's phone on the table. He ripped into all of his friends to not leave it by itself and to watch over it. On his way back from the bathroom, Andy saw something that made him want to puke. His friends were messing around and one of them shoved another over; they fell, which shook the table, which knocked his blue water bottle over. Everything happened so fast that it seemed like everything was moving in slow motion. Andrew took off running towards the table and right before he got there, his water bottle burst open. All the water and ice cubes flooded out and headed right for the phone.

The day turned inside out. For the rest of school, Andy felt terrible and was horrified thinking of what his dad would do to him when he found out he ruined his phone.

"If only the school didn't ban plastic water bottles then maybe none of this would happened." But no, Andy knew it was his fault. He shouldn't have taken his dad's phone, he should of left it right where it was by the charger in his little kitchen, which was in his little house.

* * *

The bus came to a stop. Andrew took his time arriving to his front door. He took a tiny step into his house.

"Welcome home!" his dad yelled from the upstairs.

"Hi, Dad," he replied . . .

Andy knew that the worst was yet to come.

2012

FEBRUARY 5

Ian Barritt
Age 13

Jeff Brady was a high school standout in his hometown of Ann Arbor, Michigan. His dad, who was the coach, wanted him to be just like his cousin, Tom Brady, the all time greatest NFL starting quarterback for the New England Patriots. His goals in life were to meet his cousin whom he had never met before, play in the NFL, and make his dad happy. He lived with his wealthy family, which included a loving and caring mom, one older sister attending the University of Michigan, which was the alma mater of Tom Brady. He also had a younger brother, who went to a local Ann Arbor elementary school. As the year went on, Jeff noticed that Tom and the Patriots were looking better and better.

It was just another Saturday at the football field. Ever since Jeff stepped onto the field, he was on fire. He had a total of six touchdowns, four passing, two rushing. More than ever, college scouts were showing up to his games. This was because the press found out that he was the cousin of one of the best quarterbacks of all time.

Everything felt unreal for Jeff, but it got even better. He found out that his cousin had a miraculous playoff run and was going to the Super Bowl! He and his family knew that they had to celebrate in some way. They were going to throw a super tailgate! He had a wealthy family, so he had plenty of room at his mansion-like house to throw one.

It was late afternoon. At around 3:30PM, the tailgate started. It was the middle of the winter, so the party was indoors. There were several televisions running pre-game shows. There were also many tailgate themed games. For example: corn hole and ladder toss. Jeff's family also had a few indoor grills making typical American food—hamburgers, hot dogs, chicken, etc.

It was game time! The Pats were facing the New York Giants at Lucas Oil Stadium in Indianapolis. Once the game started, everyone left the party, because it was only for the Brady's closest friends and family.

The Giants got off to a great start with nine points in the first quarter. But the Patriots and Tom Brady answered back with ten points in the second quarter, shutting the Giants out in that quarter. During halftime, the fifty-four-year-old Madonna performed for the halftime show. It was a close third quarter with the Pats scoring seven and the Giants scoring six. The score going into the fourth quarter was seventeen to fifteen. In the fourth quarter, the Giants scored six points to win, twenty-one to seventeen.

After the game, even though the Patriots lost, the Brady family still spent quality time together. Then, Jeff said, "Well, at least it wasn't a blowout." After the game, it was back to work for Jeff.

The next week, he was back at the practice field and there was a special surprise awaiting him. It was his cousin, Tom Brady. This was the first time Jeff had ever seen his cousin ever in his life. Since Jeff was also a quarterback, Tom gave Jeff some tips and techniques to Jeff. This excited Jeff very much.

In the end, even though Tom didn't win his fourth Super Bowl ring, it was still good that he met his cousin.

FEBRUARY 10

Serenity Hill
Age 13

On the cold winter day of February 10, 2012, Olivia was fast asleep. Downstairs, Olivia's mother, Maria, was planning a surprise birthday breakfast for Olivia. She was making Olivia's favorite breakfast: donuts, bacon, and hot chocolate. Then it hit Maria: she had forgotten to buy the bacon, so she asked her husband Mike, "Hey Mike, can you come downstairs please!"

"YEAH, ONE SEC," said Mike.

Mike made his way downstairs, and Maria said, "Hey, can you go to Kroger and buy some bacon? I forgot to do it."

"Sure, just let me change, and I'll be on my way," Mike said. Mike left, and it was snowing really hard. It had been a good twenty minutes and Mike hadn't walked in the door yet; Maria was getting worried! Then Maria got a call, and that's how the bad day began.

Maria answered the phone, but didn't know who it was.

"Hello," said Maria.

"Hello, this is Sheriff Jackson. Is this Maria?" asked the sheriff.

"Yes, this is Maria speaking," said Maria.

"Well ma'am, I'm calling because we got a call from someone saying there has been an accident and it appears the person in the car is your husband. We also can tell that this here was not an accident, ma'am—someone killed your husband, and it was no accident."

"What! Who could have possibly wanted my husband dead?" asked Maria.

"We are not sure, but we will be sure to find out, ma'am. We're going to need you to come down to the station to verify his body, please."

"Okay, I'm on my way, thank you."

Maria was crying and crying, and then she hung up the phone.

Olivia heard a noise and came downstairs to her mom crying. She asked, "What's wrong?" Maria was crying and crying, and couldn't stop to tell Olivia the news.

Maria said, "Olivia, I need you to sit down so I can tell you something, sweetie."

Olivia took a seat.

Maria said, "Olivia, Dad has been in an accident."

Olivia gasped, "WHAT?!"

"He did not survive, sweetie," said Maria. Olivia was crying and crying, and Maria was trying to be strong for her, but she broke down into tears. She told her, "Everything is going to be all right, I promise. Olivia, we need to go down to the police station, because I have to do something, but when we come back you can take your shower and go to bed, okay? All right, let's leave."

They headed down to the station, and Maria and Olivia entered the police station just to see Sheriff Jackson sitting down, waiting for someone to arrive and that someone was Maria.

Then Sheriff said, "Are you Maria?"

Maria said, "Yes, I am Maria, and you must be Sheriff Jackson. I got a call about something with my hus . . . husband." She started crying.

Sheriff said, "Ma'am everything will be fine, and I'm sorry for your loss, but in order for us to start the investigation we need you to make sure that body is your husband, so if you just come follow me, we can figure all of this out . . . "

Maria followed the officer to a morgue and the officer opened up one of the shelves just for her to see her husband laying on a table, dead. Maria said, "Yes, that's my husband—find the person who killed my husband, please!" Maria started crying and crying. She was overwhelmed to the point that she ran out of the morgue, took Olivia, left the station, and didn't say a word the rest of the night.

The next day was February 11, 2014. Maria was feeling horrible, but she knew that she had to wake up to get Olivia ready for school, so she got up. She called Olivia and said, "Wake up! Olivia, it's 6:30!" Olivia, who was in middle school, woke up from her rough nap, because all she could think about was her dad. *How could it be that he was dead?* She couldn't believe it. She realized it was 6:40 and she hadn't done anything. She got up and took her shower, brushed her teeth, washed her face, got dressed, did her hair, and came downstairs for breakfast. Olivia was having a hard time having an appetite after yesterday, so she didn't eat. She just walked out the house to the car without saying a word to Maria.

As Maria took Olivia to school, she tried to make conversation with Olivia, but she still wouldn't talk. Maria didn't know what to do. She was worried for Olivia, because it had only been a day since she found out about her father's death. She worried about Olivia's health and about what was racing through her mind.

Just then, Maria remembered that there was supposed to be a meet-and-greet with Whitney Houston! Maria was so happy and she shouted out, "That's it! She is in love with Whitney! This will cheer her up a little bit!" So Maria went to Ticketmaster to get two tickets for the meet-and-greet with Whitney Houston. By the time she got done, Maria was late for picking up Olivia, but she was full of excitement and couldn't wait to tell her.

Maria made it to the school fifteen minutes late. Olivia was really mad now, so it was good Maria had something to cheer her up with.

As Olivia got into the car, Maria said, "Olivia, I have something to tell you!"

Olivia said, "WHAT?"

Maria said, "Don't yell. I know that you are going through a lot, but I am too, so let's just get through this together, okay?

Olivia said, "Okay Mom, I'm sorry. I will never raise my voice again. I was wrong for that and I apologize. So, what do you need to tell me?"

Maria said, "Olivia, I know it's been rough, but I have something to cheer you up . . . surprise! Tickets to go to a meet-and-greet with Whitney Houston at 11PM tonight!"

Olivia said, "Oh my god! Oh my god! ARE YOU SERIOUS? MOM, YOU ARE THE BEST! THANK YOU, THANK YOU, THANK YOU!"

Olivia started to cry with happiness; Maria started to cry because she made her daughter happy and all she wanted was to see her daughter smiling again.

After all of the excitement, they finally made it home. Olivia went to her room to do her homework and then took a shower. Maria went into the living room and turned on the news and then everything went wrong . . . the next thing she heard was, "There has been a report that Whitney Houston has been found dead in the Beverly Hills Hotel. The cause of death is unknown at this time. We hope that family, close friends, and fans are okay. We pass on our condolences and pray for you all."

Maria's mouth dropped open and she broke down crying, because she felt as if she was failing her daughter and that was the worst feeling ever. How was she going to break the news to Olivia after she has already been hurt twice?

Then Olivia came downstairs, ready to go to the meet-and-greet. She was so excited, but then she looked at her mom and knew something was not right.

Olivia said, "Mom, what's wrong? Are you okay?"

Maria said, "Olivia, I have failed you again, I'm so sorry." Maria was crying really hard and she couldn't stop because she thought everything was her fault.

Olivia said, "Mom, what do you mean, you keep failing me . . . Mom, you got my tickets to go meet Whitney Houston!"

Maria said, "That's the problem, sweetie, there was a report telling everyone that Whit . . Whitney Houston has been found dead in her hotel just now . . . I'm so sorry!"

Maria couldn't stop crying; she felt horrible.

Then Olivia said, " Oh my gosh! Why is this happening to me?! First my dad, and now my idol. I hate my life and most of all, I hate you, Mom!"

Olivia ran upstairs in a full flood of tears. Maria was just so shocked and sad that she had failed her daughter and that her daughter would ever speak to her like that.

Maria started shaking and getting dizzy. She was getting more and more dizzy and then she blacked out and there was a big boom!

Then Olivia ran downstairs and said, "Mom? Mom? Mom? Can you hear me, Mom? Hello, MOM?"

Olivia was in full panic mode, so she called 911.

"Yes, hello, I need an ambulance at 1100 Pine Street. My mom is unconscious and she won't wake up. Please hurry up!" Olivia yelled.

Then the dispatcher said, "Ma'am, please calm down, everything will be fine. We have an ambulance on the way. They should be there shortly."

Then Olivia said, "Okay, thank you so much."

The ambulance arrived and took Maria and Olivia to the hospital as fast as possible. They arrived at the hospital and they hurried to get Maria in to be stabilized. If they didn't hurry, Maria might not make it. They got Maria to a hospital room and, by the grace of God, Maria pulled through and survived. They told Maria that the reason she blacked out was because she was under a lot of stress. Her blood pressure was way above normal and she needed to take it slow for a while.

Maria said, "I understand, but is my daughter okay? Where is my daughter?"

The nurse said, "She is outside. We will bring her in right away."

Olivia entered the room and she was crying.

"Hey, Mom," Olivia said.

"Hey darling, I love you, sweetie," Maria said.

"I love you too, Mom, and I'm sorry for what I said. I didn't mean any of it and I promise I will never disrespect you again," Olivia said.

"It's fine. It's not your fault. We both are hurting. Goodnight."

"Goodnight."

Six months after the incident . . .

After six months, Olivia and Maria's relationship had become stronger. They realized that they needed to be there for each other, because they were going through the same thing.

OCTOBER 22
Lochlann Dunlavey
Age 13

It was a cool breezy April morning in New York. We found a busy student rushing out the door to catch the bus. His name was Joseph. As he ran out of the door, the mailman stopped him in his tracks. The mailman gave him an interesting letter as he was rushing onto the bus. The letter said it was for him, so he took it with him on the bus. Joseph was wearing his favorite New York Giants shirt (he didn't realize that he was wearing that shirt or a shirt at all). Joseph played football all of his life; he was the best quarterback in his high school's history. Joseph devoted his life to playing football. He tore open the letter as soon as he got on the bus. It was an acceptance letter to one of his favorite colleges. It read: "Joseph Smith, you have been accepted into the University of Michigan." The next thing he read was better than what he read before: "You have been drafted by the University of Michigan Football team." He shot out of his seat with joy. Everyone looked at him like he was crazy; the bus was silent. After that, he sat down awkwardly. Three months later, in July, Joseph packed up and left for Michigan and headed off for college.

It was a cold October morning in downtown Ann Arbor. Joseph's alarm woke him up. There was a roaring lively city outside his dorm window. The campus of the University of Michigan was right there. He couldn't have ever imagined being here at one of his favorite colleges and being able to play for the one hundred and thirty-third Michigan team. It was October 22 in Ann Arbor. He turned on his phone and saw a news update and a Facebook update. It said "Deadly Hurricane Sandy Hits New York and destroys thousands of homes." Joseph's stomach turned into knots worrying about his parents. He tried calling them, but the phone wouldn't connect. He sat alone in his dorm, worried. Nothing mattered anymore—not football, not his friends. He felt nothing. Joseph had to do something about it. But he couldn't. He skipped school and practice that day. The worst part was football practice. He hadn't skipped practice in a long time. He tried calling them all day with the same result: no service.

Joseph had to do something. He woke up early the next day to find another news warning on his phone. It made him feel worse and worse. Joseph had no choice but to drive back home to New York to make sure that his parents were okay. He got in his car and drove all day to New York. But he was stuck. The turnpike was shut down due to the weather conditions. It took him an extra three hours to get to New York and then he got stuck again. There were three police officers guarding the only route to his parent's house. "Please let me through—I have to find my family," said Joseph with tears in his eyes. The policeman did nothing for a few seconds, and then he said, "All right, go on in. But be careful and get your family out safe." Joseph thanked the policemen as they opened their barrier. Joseph pulled up slowly and entered the hurricane-damaged town, looking for his family. It was horror in the town: water up to his ankles, buildings, such as the houses and shops in town, completely destroyed by the power of the storm, cars flipped and abandoned. As he drove his familiar route to his family's house in shock and horror, he remembered what it used to be like before the storm. Joseph was wearing his favorite New York Giants shirt with a Michigan hat. As he looked in his car window, he saw his shirt and remembered when he got his acceptance letter on one of the happiest days of his life. He remembered the birds chirping and the smell of spring in New York.

He was finally at his family's house and he got out of his truck to walked up to the door. The small blue house's windows and doors were boarded up for protection. He slowly walked up to the door and knocked on it. He waited for a few seconds until a voice came out of the door. "Who is it?"

Joseph said, "It's me, Joseph."

The voice gasped, the door opened fast, and a man and a women came out and yelled, "Son, you're here! We were so worried about you." But in reality, he was really worried about them. Joseph and his family grabbed as much stuff from the house as they could carry and packed it into the car. Then, they all drove back to Michigan. On his way back, he saw the three policemen who helped him and thanked them again.

"No problem—I see you found your family," said the policemen.

"Yes, safe and sound, just like you said," said Joseph with a smile as he pulled on to the highway that led back to Michigan.

When he arrived back in Michigan, he found a place for his parents to stay for awhile until their house was fixed. After a month or so, Joseph's parents moved back to New York to a rebuilt house. Joseph had a life ahead of him: one that he wanted his parents to be with him on, all of the way.

OCTOBER 23

Eric Salazar
Age 13

John Smith was having a great morning in the park. It was sunny and a bit windy. There were birds chirping, squirrels chattering, and you could hear the wind through the tree branches. That morning, he got a call from his cousin, who said all flights were down and he couldn't go meet him. John asked Henry, his cousin, "Why are the flights down?"

"Because of Hurricane Sandy. It's coming in real hard and everybody here is being held at the airport because it's too dangerous being in the streets."

This meeting with John and Henry had been planned for a long time, but now it was cancelled. John felt bad for Henry, since he was stuck in the airport and was in the midst of a hurricane while he was at the park on a good and sunny day. Later that day, John called Henry several times, but no one answered. He was worried because he was watching the news and the east coast looked bad. The storm was destroying it.

OCTOBER 28
Anastasia Roberson
Age 13

Taylor woke up to her phone ringing. She looked over at the clock—6:37AM. She picked up the phone and to her surprise, it was her dad. It sounded like he was crying.

She sat up, suddenly wide awake and alert. Nothing like this had ever happened before.

"Honey," he sobbed. "It's Dad." He took a deep breath, "Your mom has passed."

Taylor answered slowly, feeling like she couldn't breathe. "When? How?"

"They finally found her in the collapsed hotel that was damaged from Hurricane Sandy in New York."

"Well, what was she doing there?"

"Remember she had that job interview in New York?"

"Yeah." A long awkward silence passed.

Taylor hung up the phone suddenly, devastated. Taylor cried all day and night thinking about her mom.

A Few Months Later

Taylor had been thinking about her mom over the months, but she realized that she needed to move on to something new. She remembered that her mom went to college at University of Michigan. She decided to apply to try to transfer colleges from Central Michigan University to University of

Michigan. She moved apartments. She wanted to get her nursing degree. After getting her degree, she would move to New York and start a new life there. Taylor called her friend Kyra and told her about this idea.

"Hey, Kyra."

"Hey, how are you doing?"

"Good, and you?"

"Good . . . so you know how I started college a few months ago?"

"Yes, what about it?"

"When I finish, I want to go to New York. And start fresh there."

"What do you mean, start fresh?"

"Like . . . " Taylor paused, not knowing what to say. "I mean like, moving from here and living a different lifestyle. You know?"

"I know what you mean."

"Hey, we should travel together."

"Yes! That's a great idea!"

"I've never thought of that."

Taylor hung up the phone, suddenly excited.

Five Years Later

Taylor and Kyra both finish college at University of Michigan. They both move to New York and donate their time to the survivors of Hurricane Sandy. They help out with the community and help out with the kids and adults who have lost families from Hurricane Sandy.

DECEMBER 21

Bryan Carmona
Age 13

Chapter 1: Welcome to Michigan

December 15, 2012: One winter morning a family was having a talk and they were upset. They were eating breakfast and talking about Bryan moving to Ann Arbor, Michigan. Bryan wasn't very happy about moving, but he had to move because his family needed money, and there wasn't enough money in California where they lived. After they had their talk, he said bye to his two daughters, Luna and Sofia, and his wife, Ericka. Then he took a taxi to the airport where he would take a plane to Detroit, Michigan. Then he took a taxi to Ann Arbor, Michigan where he stayed with his friend.

He arrived at Ann Arbor, Michigan at 6:00PM. He asked his friend if he knew of any jobs available. His friend Pepe said, "Yes, where I work, there is always a job available." So Pepe took Bryan to his boss.

Bryan introduced himself, "Hi, my name is Bryan. I just got here from California and I was looking for a job. What is your name?"

"Well, hi Bryan, my name is Juan, and there surely is a job available, but it's a hard job. We are construction workers and it's really hard. It's up to you if you want to work with us," said Juan.

"Yes, I would love to work here—my family back in California really needs money."

"Okay, come to my house tomorrow morning so you can start working."

"Great, thank you so much." Pepe and Bryan got in their car, and Pepe asked Bryan if he was hungry.

Bryan said, "Yes, I am really hungry." Pepe took him to a place called "Crazy Tacos" and they ate together, like really good friends. After eating tacos, they went back home. By that time, it was 8:35PM, so Bryan went to sleep on the couch. The next morning, Pepe woke him up for work. They got dressed, ate breakfast, and while they ate breakfast, they saw the news. It said, "There is going to be an apocalypse on December 21." Bryan asked Pepe if he thought it was true.

Pepe said, "No, I don't think it is. Hopefully it doesn't happen, so don't be nervous." Bryan stayed silent for a moment. He didn't say anything for one minute—he was wondering if he should believe what the news said.

The next morning, after thinking for a long time, they got into Pepe's car and reported to Juan's house. Juan told him to go to a house and pour cement in their driveway because it was cracking. Pepe took Bryan to the house and they poured new cement in the cracks. It took two hours. Pepe called Juan. "Hey boss, we are done with the driveway, what do you want us to do next?"

"Can you guys please go to Ms. Miller's house and put drywall on the wall?"

"Yes boss," said Pepe and he drove to Ms. Miller's house. They started putting on the drywall and it took about four hours.

After they finished, Pepe called Juan. "Hey boss, we are finished with Mrs. Miller's house. What you want us to do next?" asked Pepe.

"You guys are finished for the day, so go home." Pepe and Bryan went home. They ate and did everything together.

Chapter 2: Back Home

The next few days were mostly the same, but then on December 20, 2012, Bryan woke up, ate breakfast, started thinking about what he heard in the news about the apocalypse. He started thinking about his family and he wanted to see his family so badly if the apocalypse was really going to happen. That same day was payday, so Juan gave Bryan his check. When Bryan open his check, he was excited—it was more than he could make in California in a month. He counted in total $950.00. He was so excited that he got his money. That day he made a huge decision; he decided to bring his family to Ann Arbor. So he called Erika to move to Ann Arbor. Erika said, "Yes!" with great excitement.

When Bryan's family arrived in Detroit, Michigan, Pepe and Bryan went to go pick them up. When Bryan saw his family, he was excited and he ran to hug them. It was one of those hugs where you can feel one another's heartbeat. Bryan had a tear go down his cheek. They all got into Pepe's car and headed home. During the car ride, Luna and Sofia fell asleep and Bryan asked Erika if she heard about the apocalypse that is supposed to happen tomorrow.

"Yes, you guys heard about that, too?" asked Erika.

"Yes, we did—do you really think it's true?" asked Bryan.

"I don't know what to think," said Erika. The rest of the ride they just talked about the apocalypse. When they got to Pepe's house around 9:30PM, Bryan woke Luna and Sofia up and went inside.

They ate dinner and when they finished, Sofia started to wash the dishes. Pepe left to go to his girlfriend's house. The family members were the only ones in the house. Around 11:50PM, the family cuddled in the corner waiting for what would happen at 12:00AM. Bryan kissed Luna, Sofia, and Erika, and they hugged one another and shut their eyes. At

12:00AM nothing happened. Five minutes past—nothing happened. Finally ten minutes past—nothing happened. They opened their eyes slowly. Nothing happened. It was all okay, all normal. They went outside and it was all okay—nothing happened. They went back inside, happy that nothing happened and went to sleep.

In the morning, they woke up ate and breakfast like a happy family. Pepe was still at his girlfriend's house. The rest of the day was just as scary; they just kept hugging. They all fell asleep on each other. In the morning they woke up with great energy and great excitement. They were so happy that nothing happened. They ate breakfast and they were talking like a happy family about moving to California where they really belonged. After a while, they left Michigan and moved back to California. They were so happy—they were the most happy family ever. They all loved each other. They lived happily ever after.

DECEMBER 21

Michael Rosas-Martinez
Age 13

It was 11:10AM, two minutes before 11:12, and Juan was really scared. He was on the verge of crying. In a few minutes, the world was going to end. This beautiful life as he knew it was going to end. It's 11:11:30. He only had thirty seconds of life left—but first, let's back up and see how Juan ended up here.

It was a snowy and cold morning on December 21, 2012 in Traverse City. You could hear kids playing and parents arguing. It was not the most beautiful of neighborhoods, but it was better than living under a bench on the street. This apartment building was located in a beautiful city, just not the most beautiful part of that city.

In this apartment building, in a particular apartment, there lived a man—a young man to be exact, and his name was Juan. His apartment was not the nicest place to live. You could smell rotten food and see tacos everywhere on the ground. In the corner of the room was the man, Juan. He was a short and fat man. He was just sitting there, in the corner, thinking about the day ahead and being worried. Juan got worried about everything. But right now, he was worried about something serious—or, at least, that's what he thought.

He was worried about the supposed apocalypse. The end of the world. It was supposed to happen today. Most people thought he was crazy when he tried to tell them about it. They tried to explain to him that it was all nonsense and that the world wasn't going to end, but that still didn't change his mind. Then there were other people like him who thought the world was going to end. Whenever he tried to have a serious conversation about this with them, they just changed the topic. Now he was sitting in his room thinking about all the things he regretted and things he wanted to do one last time. But it was almost impossible for him to do them. He wanted to go back home and see his family in Mexico, but it was impossible for him to get there in a few hours. It was already 5:00AM. Juan was so worried, so he just went back to sleep.

He woke up five hours later. It was 10:00AM when he checked the clock. He couldn't believe he slept for five hours. In that time he could have been doing things he liked to do, like play soccer, or he could've called his parents and family back home to talk with them one more time and tell them he loved them. There was a lot he could've done in five hours, but now he had to do them in one hour.

First, he tried calling his parents, but after ten tries of them not picking up the phone, he gave up. He then just put on his clothes and went outside for a short walk. It wasn't the most beautiful of places, but he still wanted to see it one more time before it ended as he knew it. While he was walking, he saw one of his friends. He went up to his friend, but when his friend saw him, he walked away. Juan felt like nobody wanted to see him so he just went home. When he got home, he checked what time it was; it was 11:10AM.

It was 11:10AM, a couple of minutes before 11:12, and Juan was really scared. He was on the verge of crying. In a few minutes, the world was going to end. This beautiful life as he knew it was going to end. It's 11:11:30. He only had thirty seconds of life left. He was counting down. Ten seconds left now. What was he going to? Five . . . Four . . . Three . . . Two . . . One . . . Zero . . . but suddenly, he heard a cow and started screaming and ran out of his apartment. "The world is ending!" he started shouting. "I can see Jesus, I can see Jesus, the world is ending!" and then he passed out.

What happened to Juan was very unfortunate: on his last day on Earth he started getting a little paranoid. When he started screaming, he had a heart attack and passed out. Poor Juan thought the world had ended. His last thoughts were about his family and how he never got to see them one last time, how he never got to tell them how much he loved them. When somebody saw him on the street, they called the ambulance to take him to the hospital. Then on his third day in the hospital, he woke up. When the doctors saw him, they couldn't believe it. His first words when he woke up were, "The world is ending, save yourself, save the tacos." When the doctors calmed him down and told him that the world wasn't ending, he was happy, but he also felt a little stupid. From then on, Juan decided he wasn't going to believe everything he heard. When he got out of the hospital someone told him the world was ending. He started screaming.

DECEMBER 22

Adriana Gonzalez-Figueroa
Age 13

It was December 22, 2012, exactly at 6:00AM, when Adriana got a call from her mother, who said, "Sweetheart! Sweetheart! Check the news out!" Adriana was kind of mad because her mom had just woken her up from a beautiful dream.

"Why Mom, what's going on?" Adriana was a little scared because she didn't know what was going on.

After staying in bed for two minutes, she decided to get up and turn the TV on. She saw that everybody was saying, "THE WORLD IS ENDING!!!" She had a really strange look on her face and said to her mother, "Mom? What is going on with these crazy people? Why are they saying that the world is going to end?" She was really confused at that moment. She didn't know if it was all a joke or if they were actually saying the truth.

Adriana went to the kitchen and asked her maid to please make her some pancakes with bacon and some orange juice; she loved eating that in the morning. A little while after she asked for her breakfast, she continued talking to her mom and said, "Listen Mom, I just think these people are crazy. Don't worry about it unless they continue talking about it, okay? I love you, but I have to go. Bye!"

"Bye, sweetheart."

It was noon and everything seemed to be going pretty well. Adriana decided to turn the TV on one more time—

just to check if they were still talking about "The End Of The World." When she turned the TV on, she saw that they were still talking about it, and she said to herself, *If they continue talking about it, then it's probably true.* "OH MY GOD! THE WORLD IS GOING TO END!" Adriana was really scared. She didn't know what to do, so she decided to look up "What to do when the world is going to end." She started making a safety kit: she packed food, water, a radio, money, and all the necessary things.

Adriana was really scared. She didn't know exactly what to do. Adriana grabbed all of the stuff she packed, threw it into her car, and started driving. She arrived at her mom's house, went straight inside to hug her, and said, "Mom, I love you and everything is going to be okay. Trust me." She didn't know if she really meant what she was saying because she was so scared. She called her brother, Aaron, who lived in Miami. She said that she loved him and that no matter what happened, he would always be her brother.

Six hours passed. Adriana didn't see any difference in the weather, or anything that she expected. She turned the TV on and saw that they were saying the world wasn't going to end. At first she was really mad, but then she thought about it and said, "I'm so happy nothing happened," and she hugged her mom.

ACKNOWLEDGMENTS

MG Press is eternally grateful to Frances Martin and Catherine Calabro at 826michigan for all their hard work facilitating and bringing this project to life—we couldn't have done it without their partnership. We'd also like to thank all of the volunteers at 826michigan, especially Hannah Rose Neuhauser, 826michigan Program Assistant, and everyone else who made the workshops a success: Seth Barnhill, Tom Bianchi, Chris Brudzynski, Jessi Carrothers, Barb MacKenzie, Janet Max, Abby Ruehlmann, Alyssa Selasky, Jeff Shi, Lauren Trimble, and Dani Vignos. And a huge thanks, too, to Cammie Finch for her enthusiasm and tireless effort on this project from its very inception. Thanks are also in order for Lauren Crawford, for creating a beautiful cover to envelop the words of these students. Most of all, for the eighth-grade students at Scarlett Middle School and their teachers, Sal Barrientes and Ellen Daniel, for growing the next generation of Midwestern voices.

ABOUT MG PRESS

MG Press is a micro-press devoted to publishing a small number of titles each year. An extension of the literary journal Midwestern Gothic, MG Press retains the same core values: shining a spotlight on Midwest authors by focusing on works that showcase all aspects of life—good, bad, or ugly.

The authors and books we choose to work with exemplify these traits; they are representatives of the Midwest, and aim to celebrate what makes the Midwest such a unique place, highlighting our mythologies, stories, and culture that the world may be missing out on.

ABOUT 826MICHIGAN

826michigan is a nonprofit organization dedicated to supporting students ages 6 to 18 with their creative and expository writing skills, and to helping teachers inspire their students to write. Our services are structured around the understanding that great leaps in learning can happen with one-on-one attention, and that strong writing skills are fundamental to future success. With this in mind, we provide after-school tutoring, evening workshops, in-school residencies, help for English language learners, and assistance with student publications. All our programs are challenging and enjoyable, and ultimately strengthen each student's power to express ideas effectively, creatively, confidently, and in his or her individual voice.

Tutoring is at the Heart of It
Our method is simple: we assign free tutors to students so that the students can get one-on-one help. It is our understanding that great advancement in English skills and comprehension can be made within hours if students are given concentrated help from knowledgeable tutor-mentors. We offer free tutoring four days a week at both our writing lab at 115 E. Liberty Street in downtown Ann Arbor (just inside the Liberty Street Robot Supply & Repair) and at 20 N. Washington Street in downtown Ypsilanti (just inside Beezy's Cafe).

Workshops
We offer a number of free workshops taught by professional art-

ists and our talented volunteers. From comic books to screenplays, bookmaking to radio, our wide variety of workshops are perfect for passionate writers of all ages and interests.

In-School Projects
Our trained volunteers go into local public schools every day to support teachers with their classroom writing assignments. Based on the teacher's curriculum, assignments range from writing tales to crafting five-paragraph essays.

Field Trips
We want to help teachers get their students excited about writing, while helping students be better able to express their ideas. We welcome teachers to bring their classes in for field trips during the school day. A group of volunteers is on hand at every field trip, whether we are helping to generate new material or revise works-in-progress. Our most popular field trip is our Storytelling & Bookmaking workshop, which culminates in a book for each student to take home.

Our Store
The Liberty Street Robot Supply & Repair, a one-stop shop for robots and robot owners and enthusiasts alike, is designed to inspire creativity and advertise our programs to the community. Come visit us at 115 East Liberty Street in downtown Ann Arbor. All proceeds from our store directly fund our programs. Onward robots!

CPSIA information can be obtained at www.ICGtesting.com
Printed in the USA
LVOW10s1711240415

435997LV00003B/68/P